I0628053

# What Bad Bitches Do 2

Lock Down Publications and
Ca$h Presents

# What Bad Bitches Do 2
## A Novel by Aryanna

# Lock Down Publications

P.O. Box 870494
Mesquite, Tx 75187

**Visit our website**
www.lockdownpublications.com

First Edition August 2018
Printed in the United States of America

*This is a work of fiction. Names, characters, places, and incidents either are products of the author's imagination or are used fictitiously. Any similarity to actual events or locales or persons, living or dead, is entirely coincidental.*

**Lock Down Publications**
**Like our page on Facebook: Lock Down Publications @**
www.facebook.com/lockdownpublications.ldp
Cover design and layout by: **Dynasty Cover Me**
Book interior design by: **Shawn Walker**
Edited by: **Jill Alicea**

# Stay Connected with Us!

Text **LOCKDOWN** to 22828 to stay up-to-date
with new releases, sneak peeks, contests and more…

# Submission Guideline.

Submit the first three chapters of your completed manuscript to ldpsubmissions@gmail.com, subject line: Your book's title. The manuscript must be in a .doc file and sent as an attachment. The document should be in Times New Roman, double-spaced and in size 12 font. Also, provide your synopsis and full contact information. If sending multiple submissions, they must each be in a separate email.

Have a story but no way to send it electronically? You can still submit to LDP/Ca$h Presents. Send in the first three chapters, written or typed, of your completed manuscript to:

LDP: Submissions Dept
Po Box 870494
Mesquite, Tx 75187

*DO NOT send original manuscript. Must be a duplicate.*

Provide your synopsis and a cover letter containing your full contact information.

Thanks for considering LDP and Ca$h Presents.

# ARYANNA

# Chapter 1
## Ivy

The pistol in my hand jumped to life as my feet moved in Ebony's direction, but I couldn't tell the difference between my gunfire and the surround sound of shots coming from every direction. The smart thing for me to do was to move away from the chaotic gunfight, but this wasn't about being smart. It was about survival.

"Ebony, shoot!" I yelled, still pulling the trigger of my own gun and running in her direction. I don't know what was running through this bitch's mind, but she was frozen in place, leaving Justice and me to return fire on José and his goons. To my delight I heard José scream, which meant one of my bullets found its mark, but that victory was short-lived because Justice suddenly went down, and that left Ebony out in the open.

"Get down!" I screamed, diving and tackling her.

"Bitch, get off me!" she hollered.

"I'm trying to help your dumb ass, so shut up and come on," I demanded, grabbing her hand and pulling her behind her truck to use it as a shield.

"Awwww *fuck*!" she screamed, in pain.

It was way too dark to see where she was shot, but the blood soaking through her T-shirt indicated she'd definitely been hit.

"Just get away from me, or fucking shoot me! This shit is all *your* fault, bitch!" she raged, grabbing her right side.

I could tell she wasn't about to go anywhere with me willingly, and given everything I'd done, I couldn't exactly blame her. This wasn't about us right now though. It was obvious to me that the Sinola Cartel had done its best to play us against each other so they could pick up the pieces, which made *them* my enemy, not her. Ebony might not be my sister anymore, but it wasn't right to make her baby pay for that.

"Just keep your head down," I said. The gunfire seemed to be happening all around us, but it wasn't as close as it had been. I took a deep breath before leaving the safety of our temporary hiding spot and making a mad dash for my car. I felt the heat of bullets whizzing past me, but I made it to the driver's seat of the Rolls Royce Phantom without getting hit.

"I-vy," my dad called weakly from the backseat,

"Hold on, Dad, I'm getting us the fuck out of here," I said, starting the engine, throwing the car into gear, and taking off. Immediately, bullets began raining on the cotton candy blue paint job, making me glad I'd ordered the car built heavily armored. Common sense said to keep driving right past Ebony's truck, but I still found myself sliding my car to a stop and hopping out to save her ungrateful ass.

"Come on," I said, grabbing her under her arms and pulling her around the front of my car to the passenger side door.

"Get the fuck off me!" she yelled, trying to fight her way out of my arms.

"Bitch, if you keep struggling, I'ma shoot you my goddamn self! I'm trying to save you and that baby," I said, pulling her faster. Once I had her in the car, I raced back to the driver's side, but the sight of Justice crawling towards me in the dirt stopped me from getting in. Him showing up with Ebony, obviously choosing her side in this ongoing war, meant I didn't owe him shit. Did that mean I could leave him for dead?

"Fuck," I said under my breath, reaching back in my car long enough to grab my pistol. I fired all four shots in the general direction of where I'd last spotted José before weaving my way towards Justice.

"I should leave your ass here," I said, bending down and allowing him to put his weight on me to support his wounded leg.

"I l-love you too," he stammered, moving as fast as his good leg would carry him.

I was about to put him in my car with the other wounded traitor when something occurred to me.

"Where's Marissa?" I asked, looking first at Ebony's truck and then at Justice's truck parked directly behind hers.'

"In my truck," he replied.

"You're gonna have to drive then," I said, helping him to his driver's side door. Once he was behind the wheel I ran back to my car, dove in, and put the pedal to the floor.

"This-this shit *hurts*!" Ebony cried through gritted teeth.

"I'm getting you to the hospital, just hold on."

"My-my mom. We have to go back-."

"Justice has your mom," I said, checking my rearview mirror to see that he was still behind me. Of all the ways this night could've ended, I never would've thought that I'd be the one helping to save Ebony and her mom. True enough we'd been family once, closer than twins, but in the last three months, all that had changed drastically. We'd gone from two college kids to two rivals fighting for control of the street empire that our fathers had built together. Gunfights and clandestine meetings weren't how we lived our lives, but times had changed. For me they were on the verge of changing again because my heart didn't hold the same hate that it once had for Ebony. She hadn't killed my father, and she could've. The fact that I'd had both her mother and her baby daddy as my bargaining chips didn't change the fact that I'd put a bullet through her father's brain. She could've easily taken her revenge, but she didn't. The war between us had been sparked by her father's betrayal of my father, but I now understood that the Sinola Cartel added fuel to the spark. It was them who deserved my hurt and anger, not the woman bleeding all over my Italian leather.

"We're almost there," I said, finally coming out of the rural area we'd been in and into the city lights.

"Hurry up. *Fuck*, this shit hurts!" she exclaimed.

"Don't think about it; focus on something else," I said lamely.

"Bitch, fuck you! I should've shot your ass when I had the chance."

"Yeah, maybe, but your ass really should've *ducked* when all the fucking shooting started. You ain't no superwoman, bitch," I said, fishtailing through a red light.

"Ivy. I-vy," my dad called again.

"It's okay, Daddy, I'm getting us to the hospital," I said, looking at him in the rearview mirror. I wanted to cry with relief and sadness. I was so thankful he was alive, but the man in my backseat was only a shell of the Solomon Black I'd grown up with. My dad was larger than life, my very own superhero, and hopefully it wasn't too late to get him back to who he was. After the longest ten minutes of my life, I slid to a stop in front of the emergency room entrance and hopped out.

"Help! I need help!" I screamed, running around to Ebony's side of the car. Immediately, three nurses rushed out to see what the commotion was.

"Ma'am, what is it?"

"Two gunshot victims, and one more on the way," I said, pulling Ebony out of the car. Under the bright lights of the emergency room entrance, I could see that her shirt was completely soaked with blood, and she was on the verge of losing consciousness. The nurses said the same thing because they began barking out orders that brought more people running with stretchers and IV stands. After handing Ebony over, I went straight for my father and helped him out of the backseat onto a waiting stretcher.

"Ivy - "

"It's okay, Dad, I'll be right there," I said, squeezing his hand and kissing his forehead. I couldn't hold in my tears any longer, and I saw that he was crying too.

Two nurses quickly whisked the occupied stretchers into the ER just as Justice slid the black Escalade to a stop behind my car.

"Here's your other gunshot victim," I said, rushing to help him from the truck.

"She's in the backseat," Justice whispered before the nurses took him from me and wheeled him inside.

Standing outside by myself, I realized that I had a tough decision to make. With all my heart I wanted to be in that hospital seeing to my father's treatment, but if I didn't deal with Marissa, what would she say to the cops once they arrived? I couldn't go to jail, not right now, so that only left one alternative. Looking around quickly, I went to the back of Justice's truck, where I found Marissa still unconscious, sprawled across the backseat. I pulled her out and carried her around to my car, hurriedly pushing her in before anyone spotted me. I thought my father being alive meant I might be able to go back to the girl I used to be, but that dream was for tomorrow. For now, I had to hold shit down, like a real bitch would.

# ARYANNA

## Chapter 2
## Ebony
## Two days later

Awakening to the sounds of hospital machines beeping and breathing for me was enough to send a fresh dose of panic rushing into my veins, but it was no match for the dope I was on. My thoughts were surprisingly clear and I remembered everything that had gotten me to this situation, which should've been more motivation to get up. I just couldn't.

"Are you awake?" I heard a voice ask from the shadows of my hospital room. For a split second my panic turned to ice cold fear, but I quickly realized who the voice belonged to.

"Justice," I slurred, squinting in the direction that I thought I heard the voice come from.

"I'm here. How are you feeling?" he asked, rolling into my view.

"Wheel-chair," I said slowly.

"Yeah, but only because I got shot in the leg. I'm not paralyzed."

"That's-that's good. Where's Mom?" I asked, remembering that we'd been doing a prisoner exchange before all hell broke loose.

"She's safe," Justice replied.

"Where?" I persisted.

"Ivy took her back to her hotel and left her there, unharmed."

It was hard to believe that the evil bitch didn't kill my mother out of sheer spite. I couldn't yet make sense out of her saving our lives, but I had no doubt that the bitch was up to something.

"Where's Rock?" I asked in a stronger voice. At first Justice didn't answer, but the look on his face was easy to read.

"J?" I said.

"Ivy still has him."

Hearing this forced me to close my eyes again as tears slid soundlessly down my face.

"She's not gonna hurt him. He's just insurance right now," Justice said reassuringly.

"How do you know?" I asked, still not opening my eyes.

"Because I talked to her."

Hearing this declaration did make me open my eyes and lock them on his face, hoping to discover that he'd just lied to me. "You talked to her? I asked in disbelief.

"Yeah. E.B, I don't know what happened before I got here, but it's obvious to me that Ivy still loves you. She saved all of us."

"It was her fault we were *there*," I said, becoming angry by his sudden defense of Ivy.

"I'm not saying she's without blame. I'm saying she could've left our asses for dead and she didn't, and that should count for something."

"That don't count for *shit*, because my dad is still dead, and - "

My rant was interrupted by a short, blond man in a white lab coat suddenly coming through the door to my room. "Ms. Dahl, my name is Doctor Crith. How are you feeling?"

"Like I've been shot and doped up," I replied sarcastically.

"Well, unfortunately, both of those things did happen, and it's normal to feel incredibly groggy after multiple procedures."

"Multiple procedures? Why did I have more than one?" I asked, fear quickly replacing the anger I'd just been feeling.

When Justice and the doctor exchanged a look, I felt my heart snap because I knew what neither of them wanted to say. "The baby?" I asked softly, locking eyes with Justice and finding a sympathy there that I knew the doctors didn't possess.

"I'm sorry, Ms. Dahl. It's almost impossible to save any fetus when the mother suffers a gunshot wound to the stomach. The good news is that I did a full exam on you after surgery, and what happened won't prevent you from carrying another child to full term."

I knew his words were meant to inspire hope, but there was no consolation prize for losing my baby, and hope didn't stop my tears from flowing.

"Give us a minute, doc," Justice said.

Through my underwater view I saw the man retreat silently the way he'd come, but it wasn't until the door closed that I gave myself to the gut-wrenching sobs that rocked my body. Even though my pregnancy hadn't been planned, I'd loved my baby with all my heart, and in the blink of an eye, I'd lost everything. Knowing that I might've lost the last part of the man I loved too made me cry harder, almost to the point where I thought I would vomit at any moment.

"I'm so sorry, E.B.," Justice said sincerely, rolling his wheelchair right next to my bed and taking my hand in his.

Nothing he could say would fix the giant hole in my heart, but part of me was grateful to have someone to go through this with. Like a good friend and a real man he let me sob, ugly cry, and blubber like a fool without saying another word for the next hour, until I was finally able to reel my emotions in somewhat.

"I n-need to get out of here," I said, wiping the tears from my eyes and the snot from my nose.

"I don't know when you'll be discharged, but - "

"I don't give a fuck about being discharged or any of that shit! I *need to get the* fuck out of here!" I growled, snatching my hand away from his and pulling my IV out to show my determination.

"Okay, chill, I'll get you out of here. Let me go make the necessary phone calls and arrange our ride, and in the meantime, you lay there and don't do no dumb shit. I know you're hurt and upset, but you did still suffer a gunshot wound, which means you're not at one hundred percent. You called me down here to help you, so let me do that," he requested reasonably.

I felt like my skin was crawling with each passing moment I had to stay in this hospital bed, but I knew at the very least, I had to wait on a ride. "Hurry up," I said impatiently.

Without another word he rolled himself from the room, leaving me alone with the annoying sounds of the hospital machines and the ghost of my lost child. I put my hands under my hospital gown and onto my stomach because it didn't seem real that my baby could just be *gone*. I couldn't understand why God would give me this gift and responsibility only to snatch it away so quickly. It wasn't really God's fault though, was it? The world was controlled by evil, and Ivy was a part of that evil. I didn't know why she decided to have a sudden change of heart and be helpful, but it was too little too late as far as I was concerned. That bitch had to pay for all that she'd taken from me. It was just that simple. The only question now was, how would I make her pay? Turning my thoughts to answering that question helped to pass the time in a less stressful way, and before I knew it, Justice was being wheeled back into my room.

"Why you ain't dressed yet?" he asked immediately.

"Because I don't have any clothes, Negro."

"Oh, your sister brought you a bag yesterday," the nurse who'd been pushing Justice's wheelchair said.

"My sister? I don't have a sister," I replied, going from confused to angry as it became clear who the nurse was referring to.

"Oh, well that's how the young lady introduced herself. Here's the bag she left," the nurse said, taking a brown leather Louis Vuitton bag from the wooden closet by the front door, and setting it on the bed beside me.

"I'll give you a couple minutes to get dressed, but I'll only be outside if you need me," Justice offered.

"I can help if - "

"No thank you, nurse, I can manage," I said, still staring at the bag next to me. It erased all doubt that the young lady the nurse had referred to was, in fact, Ivy, because I recognized the bag as one I'd given to her at her sweet sixteen birthday party. I had a matching one - or at least, I'd *had* a matching one before the bitch burned down my house.

Even after the room was cleared, it still took me a minute to pull the bag towards me and open it. The first thing I saw was a little black Gucci dress that brought back another memory. Ivy and I had worn matching black dresses as a political statement during a President Trump event we'd crashed with a few friends from the Black Lives Matter organization. I doubted she put it in the bag for nostalgic reasons though. More likely it was proper morning attire. Surprisingly, I didn't take it as her being a smart ass, but more so an attempt at being thoughtful. Digging deeper in the bag, I found clean underwear and a pair of black flats to go with my outfit. Underneath all the clothing lay two more items that caused all types of questions. The first item was a phone with a Post-It note on the screen that read "you know the code". I quickly turned it on and tapped my birthday in to bypass the security measures that were in place to keep everyone except me out. The phone was obviously brand new, but there was a text message waiting for me from a number I didn't recognize. After bracing myself for the bullshit, I read it slowly.

*I know I can't ask you to let bygones be bygones, but you're gonna have to if you wanna live. That's not a threat either. The reality is that we now have a common enemy to deal with. We could point the finger at each other for all the shit that's happened, but we both know that a certain group of people motivated by its own self-serving interests caused all this shit to happen. They can't get away with that. I'm not suggesting that we join forces because I can't eliminate them on my own. I'm suggesting it because you're basically a sitting duck. Even with Justice and his people behind you, you're still no match for what's coming your way. By now it's obvious to you that Rock has lost his backing too, but that's tomorrow's problem. Today's problem is that, whether you like it or not, you're still in the middle of a war, and not even your grief can slow down the events that are in motion. I know you probably hate me, and I deserve it, but that doesn't make anything I'm saying less true. The wolves are coming, Ebony. Let me help you.*

At first I couldn't believe the nerve of this bitch suggesting we join forces. She *had* to be out of her rabbit-ass mind! Right? If I was looking at this situation from an emotional standpoint, then she was definitely out of her mind. However, if I were simply evaluating the situation logically, then I'd have to admit that the Sinaloa Cartel coming after me was all bad right now. I knew Justice had goons that would ride for him, but would they be enough? And even though it pained me in more than one way to admit it, Ivy was right about Rockafella's people too, because if they were still loyal to him, they wouldn't have turned him over to her. Ivy had the

Gulf Cartel and the Hoovers behind her, not to mention her father's connections. She would survive, and she was now offering me the safety of her umbrella. Part of my brain insisted it was a trick and that the bitch couldn't be trusted, but the part of my brain rooted in self-preservation was already working overtime.

Putting the phone aside, I reached into the bag and pulled out the last item. I couldn't remember the last time I'd seen it, but the weight of the nickel plated forty-five in my hand was comforting. Maybe Ivy was right. That didn't mean I couldn't settle the score with her after.

# ARYANNA

# Chapter 3
## Ivy

"I don't like being summoned," I said, walking into the living room of my townhouse, where I found Hoover Slim sitting on my couch.

"I don't like summoning you, but for obvious reasons, you know it ain't safe to talk on the phone," he replied.

He was damn sure right about that because the last forty-eight hours of my life had been filled with endless police activity. Getting my father proper treatment had been my main priority, which meant there was no way to keep his return to the land of the living a complete secret. Of course, with his return came the questions about where he'd been, who had taken him, and more importantly, how did *I* get him back. Thankfully, our lawyer, Joey, was on his job and handling the law enforcement circus, but it was evident that they weren't leaving town without answers. I'd already had my dad moved back to his house after flying in the best medical staff available to be on-call, in hopes of giving him more privacy. The Feds were still watching though, so I had to move carefully.

"What's so important that I had to rush right over here?" I asked, sitting on the loveseat across from him. I didn't miss the way his eyes tracked my movements, or the heat coming from his stare when I crossed my legs beneath my off-white knee length Zac Posen dress. My purpose for being here was all business, and if he knew like I did, then his would be too.

"There's a few things we need to deal with before I head back to Houston, mainly the nigga that's still bound and gagged in the other room," he replied.

"I'll take care of him when - "

"Nah, you won't, actually. I've talked it over with Gangsta Bit and we've decided to handle the situation ourselves, for personal reasons. I'm sure you can understand that."

I didn't understand shit about gang life, but it was clear by the look on Hoover Slim's face that something bad was in store for Rockafella. I really shouldn't have cared given everything that had gone down, especially since he helped to shoot up my mother's funeral. At the same time, I was trying to repair things with Ebony, and sending her man to his death wasn't helping my cause.

"Rock is my only leverage right now. I can't give that up," I said reasonably.

"You're talking like this was a request I'm making. It's not. Gangsta Bit runs Global Gangsta, and since Rock pledged his allegiance to that organization, that makes him property of Global Gangsta. Out of loyalty for your man, I made it to where you could use Rock as a means to an end, but the time for that has passed. You got your dad back, so be grateful, but don't act like you still need Rock for your war with Ebony because you saved her life. It's clear where you two stand now, so I'm taking Rock with me."

I could literally feel and taste the blood in my mouth from the hole I was biting in my tongue. I wanted to clap back at this lanky nigga with all 5'4", 150 pounds of me, but I maintained my composure because even through my anger I could see he was right. It was obvious I wasn't about to win this argument, which meant that I had to figure out how to break the news to Ebony.

"What else do we need to address before you leave?" I asked, hoping to move this meeting along.

"We need to discuss what to do about Big Cuzz and - "

"I've got that taken care of," I said quickly.

"Oh yeah? And how is that?"

"He'll be out on bond by tomorrow and we'll figure the rest out from there. I'm putting all my dad's connections to use," I replied confidently.

"That's good. I think the witness is gonna have a change of heart, so once he's out, he shouldn't be going back in. Don't ask any unnecessary questions," he said, holding his hand up to wave off whatever I was gonna say.

I closed my mouth, realizing that knowing too much made me a liability and not an asset. "It seems like yo' expectations got shit under control, but there's something else we need to discuss. I'm pretty sure this war with the Sinaloa Cartel is only getting started," I said.

"Do you think that's wise?"

"I think it's unavoidable. It's obvious that they were intending to take over everything my dad and Jacob built, which of course affects you and your people. They're not gonna stop now, especially with one of their top men falling in that shit show the other night. I don't think they'll attack me directly right now because of all the attention surrounding my dad, but Ebony is a sitting duck, and they probably understand my attention being divided right now."

"Okay, all that sounds true. So what's your plan?" he asked.

"I'm working on that, but I think you need to be ready for an attack on our mutual interests."

For a moment he said nothing and simply stared at me thoughtfully. I didn't know what he was thinking, but at least his eyes didn't have that hungry predator look from earlier.

"You know, when we found out your dad was alive, I wondered what would happen once he returned home. I mean, I knew it would take time for him to heal, but I wondered if he would reclaim the throne once he was able to. I know now that ain't gonna happen because there's a new ruler, but I wonder if you see it in yourself yet. If you do, then you'll understand that saving Ebony didn't salvage your relationship. The closer you keep her, the more you're courting karma, and believe me, karma is a bitch that not even you can handle. I'll get Rock and see myself out," he said, standing up and leaving the room.

Even though he wasn't here, his words were still bouncing off the walls and ringing in my ears. Was he right? Was I on my way to becoming a queen pin? That question required more reflection than I had time for right now, and all I knew for certain at this point was that I would do what was necessary to protect my family.

While waiting for Hoover Slim to carry Rock's unconscious body out to his truck, I contemplated what my next move would be. I knew I didn't have much time before the next round of bullets was exchanged, but one thing I was certain of was that I needed to get Big out before that happened. After making sure my house was no longer an active crime scene, I reset my alarm and headed out the door and back to my parents' house. Despite the fact that Hoover Slim was headed out of town, there was still a Range Rover following my car, but I wasn't mad at the extra security. I'd already turned my parents' house into an armed fortress with round the clock armed guards both inside and walking the grounds. I was seriously contemplating building a brick wall around every square inch of property. Even though my experience with the street life was limited, I understood that there was no such thing as too much security.

I made the drive back to my parents' house in an hour, making sure to keep my eyes open for anyone following or tracking my movements. I didn't think I was too paranoid because I knew without a doubt that my enemies were out there, lurking. As I walked into the house, my mind was focused on business and the next moves that needed to be made, but first I had to check on my dad.

"How is he?" I asked the guard sitting outside his room. Normally my dad would be upstairs in the master suite he shared with my mom, but both his health and security needs had forced me to set him up in a room on the first floor. I actually liked it because it was just down the hall from his office, which I'd been using in his absence.

"He's okay. It's been quiet. Nobody in or out except the nurse and doctor."

"Has there been any activity anywhere on the property?" I asked.

"No ma'am. I've had all of my men on high alert, and I'm keeping them on eight hour rotations so fatigue doesn't set in."

"That's why I chose your security firm, James. You're the best at what you do," I said, opening the door to my dad's room and stepping inside. Given my recently made connections in the underworld, I'd had the option to have my dad surrounded with real goons, but given the Feds interest in us right now, I thought legal shooters was smarter. I crept through the door, expecting to find my father sleeping, but his eyes were locked on mine as soon as I became visible.

"Hi Daddy," I said, smiling despite the heartbreak I felt at seeing him looking so fragile and helpless.

"Hey baby," he replied, his voice stronger than I'd anticipated.

I crossed the room and sat in the chair that was next to his bed, careful not to disturb the machines he was hooked up to. They were just a precaution to make sure he was getting the vital fluids and nutrients that his body needed in order to heal and fight off the infection he'd gotten from an improperly treated gunshot wound. There was no doubt that he would live, but his paralysis was likely permanent. That was a hard pill for either of us to swallow

"How are you feeling?" I asked softly.

"Thankful to be alive. I'm more worried about you than anything though."

"I'm fine, Daddy, you don't have to worry about me," I said, smiling reassuringly.

"Don't I? I never wanted this life for you, sweetheart, and now you're in deeper than I ever thought possible. I saw the video of Jacob."

I didn't really know what to say to that. I was definitely surprised that José had showed my dad the video of me killing his oldest friend - Ebony's dad - but I didn't see judgement in my dad's eyes.

"Once I figured out what he'd done, I didn't see another way out for him. There was no way I'd let him or anyone else take over what you built, Dad, I couldn't do that."

"But this ain't your *life*, Ivy. You're better than this, better than the bullshit that comes with this," he replied passionately.

"How can you say that? You and Mom didn't raise me to believe that I was better than you or anyone else walking this Earth. You kept me firmly rooted in reality, and the reality is that the world ain't built on rainbows and horseshoes. It's built on blood, sweat, and tears, and I'm not above any of that."

"You could've been. Your mom and I wanted you to be," he replied, defeat lacing his words.

Even though I know he couldn't feel me, I still took his hand in my own. "Daddy, I'm your daughter, and I'm *proud* of that because you're such an incredible man. I know this isn't what you wanted for my life, but this is God's plan and not mine, or yours. We can't change the way things are now, so we just have to accept it and keep moving forward."

We sat in silence while my dad looked at the ceiling, maybe seeing things as they used to be.

"Did your mom know about you?" he asked.

It had been so hard to break the news to him about my mom dying from a heart attack once he was kidnapped, but he'd been asking for her. It hit him just as hard as I'd expected, but some part of him had already accepted that she would be gone before her time because the cancer had returned.

"No, Mom didn't know anything. I'm not sure I could've been as coldhearted as I needed to be if she would've been around," I admitted. My response to his question brought a long sigh from his mouth, but I couldn't tell if it was one of relief or acceptance.

"So what's going on now?" he asked.

"Dad, I don't wanna talk business."

"Well, we damn sure ain't about to sit here and discuss my inability to feel anything below my neck," he said seriously.

He'd never been the type to throw pity parties or feel sorry for himself, so I shouldn't have expected anything different now.

"I'm anticipating the Sinaloa Cartel coming after us and Ebony, probably Ebony first. I've warned her, but I don't know if she'll accept my help," I said honestly.

"If she doesn't, you can't worry about that right now. You've gotta get with Big's people so we have some type of backing, because - "

"I'm already on that, plus the Gulf Cartel is behind us," I said.

"The Gulf Cartel? When did they become our allies?"

"When I started purchasing metric tons of their dope and distributing it all across North America," I stated with a shy smile. When I looked into my dad's eyes this time I saw something that made me feel warm inside. I saw respect.

"Seems like you were really busy during my absence. So maybe you should catch me up on exactly how well you've handled the family business."

## Chapter 4
## Ebony

"Thank God you're alive!" My mom said, as soon as I was wheeled through her hotel room door.

"I feel the same way about you," I replied, accepting her hug and squeezing her as tightly as my injury would allow. We stayed locked in each other's embrace for a long moment, both of us crying silent tears for reasons that we were too emotional to verbalize. None of the differences we'd had, not even the disagreement about whether or not I should have my baby, mattered right now. We'd both lost so much already, and I was simply glad to still have my mom.

"Are you okay?" I asked, pulling back so I could look her over from head to toe.

"I got a lump on my head, but I'm okay. I'm more worried about you...and the baby."

I could clearly read the question in her eyes, and I felt the lump in my throat from immediately. I couldn't give words to my pain, but I did manage to shake my head sadly as more tears slid down my face.

"Aww, baby, I'm so sorry," she said, pulling me back into her arms.

The comfort I felt in my mother's arms was parallel to none and I felt safe enough to come all the way unglued, but now wasn't the time for that.

"Mom, you remember Justice," I said, pulling away again and looking up into her blue-green eyes. I watched her look past me to the man who'd wheeled me into the room, and I could tell she recognized him a little.

"Justice...you were around when Ebony was a kid, right?"

"Yes. It's good to see you again, Mrs. Dahl. I wish it was under better circumstances, and I'm sorry for your loss," he replied respectfully.

"Thank you. I take it you're here because of everything that's going on."

"Ebony called and I came," he replied simply.

"I'm thankful. Come in, come in," she said, backing up to allow us full entry into her room. She still had the whole top floor of the Marriot in Houston rented out since we still didn't have a home, thanks to Ivy's treachery. I didn't know how long she planned on us staying here since money wasn't an option, but I knew we needed to start over and put down new roots.

"Did you get yourself checked out, Mom?" I asked, moving slowly from my wheelchair to the couch next to her.

"I'm *fine*, Ebony, really. Besides, I haven't really felt like leaving the hotel."

Knowing what she'd endured made that statement understandable because my mom came from a privileged background that didn't tolerate street shit. She was a wealthy white woman and *not* about that life.

"Why haven't you hired some security people?" I asked.

"I plan to. I just wanted to talk with you first because I know Ivy still has Rock. I didn't wanna do something that would cause her to do something to him because it's *clear* the bitch is unstable."

"On that we agree. I think security is necessary though," I said.

"Why? She *can't* be still trying to kill you after she just saved your life," she stated, disbelief evident on her face.

"No, I don't think she is right now, but she seems to believe the cartel is still coming after us. I think she could be full of shit and working an angle."

"I don't think so," Justice interjected, sitting beside me on the couch.

"Well, Justice, I'm not sure how much Ebony told you about the new and improved Ivy, but that bitch can't be trusted," my mom said, anger and bitterness lacing her words.

I know no matter what happened, my mother would never forget seeing the video of my dad's execution, any more than she'd forgive Ivy for pulling the trigger. Despite understanding how the cartel had played our families against each other, the fact still remained that Ivy killed my father, my mother's husband.

"I'm well aware of the situation, Mrs. Dahl, and I've heard it from both sides. I'm not here to make excuses for anything Ivy did, but the fact that the Sinaloa cartel played everybody for their own personal gain can't be ignored. I believe Ivy when she says that the cartel will attack again. My homies had to go back to Dallas, but they'll be back up here in a couple days. Until then, I suggest that some form of security is hired because it's better to be safe than sorry - unless you're comfortable accepting help from Ivy," Justice replied.

"I'll make the calls in the morning," my mom said quickly.

"It won't be like this forever, Mom, eventually shit will calm down."

"How can you be so sure?" She asked.

"Because Ivy has proven in more ways than one that she'll do whatever it takes to hold onto what she has. So either she'll stop the wolves at the door or she'll become their next meal. I don't see how we lose," I replied coldly. Truthfully, I wanted to be the one to end that bitch's life, but I'd lost a lot fighting that uphill battle. One thing I'd learned was that dead was dead, regardless of how it happened.

"I'm surprised the hospital released you so soon," my mom said, changing the subject.

When I didn't respond to her comment immediately, I felt the familiar heat of her stare trying to lift the side of my face so she could peek at my brain.

"They did discharge you, didn't they?" she asked.

When I finally looked at her, I could tell that any bullshit was gonna be met with anger.

"They didn't discharge her, but I spoke to the doctor to assess the risk before we left, and I have her prescriptions. We both felt that staying in Fort Worth wasn't a good idea right now," Justice said.

"Okay, but won't the police be looking for Ebony? I know they question all gunshot victims as a matter of procedure. They'll probably be looking for you too, if that limp is any indication."

I hadn't thought about that part of the equation, but it was too late to go back now, and I wouldn't anyway.

"Neither one of us is obligated to answer any questions, and if they try to press the issue, that's what the lawyers are for. Besides, Ivy took care of that particular problem," Justice replied casually.

Hearing this caused me to turn and look at him because this was definitely news to my ears. The look he returned was unapologetic, and knowing him, I shouldn't have expected it to be.

"She's being *way* too helpful not to be up to something," my mom said cynically.

"Let's agree to disagree," Justice replied.

I was in no mood to argue or watch an argument because I could feel the pain in my stomach coming back.

"Mom, if that's one less thing we have to worry about, then that's good. Tomorrow we'll start to figure out what our next move should be because right now I need a hot bath and another dose of my medications," I said, rising slowly from the couch and sitting back in the wheelchair.

"Okay, baby, but I want you in the room adjacent to mine in case you need anything. Justice, you can take any room you want on this floor."

"Mom, I'll be fine," I said, pulling the pistol from underneath the cushion of my wheelchair so she could see it.

"And I'm not leaving her side," Justice chimed in, standing up and moving slowly to stand behind the wheelchair.

The way her eyes locked on the gun in my hand gave her face a haunted expression, but I knew it was because she recognized the gun and not because she was scared. She should've recognized the gun. It was hers, and it was the twin to the one that had killed my father. Ivy had the other one.

"Is-is that mine or - "

"It's yours, Mom. Ivy left it for me in the bag she brought to the hospital," I said quickly.

"Oh. Well it's good that you have protection, and I guess I'll see you both in the morning," she replied softly.

My heart ached for my mom, not just because of the loss we'd suffered, but because of the guilt I felt for bringing so much chaos to her door. She'd tried telling me that I was in too deep, and me ignoring those words had contributed to her kidnapping. I didn't know how I would've lived with it if my actions had resulted in her death.

"Can we have breakfast together?" I asked, hoping to lighten the mood.

"I'd like that," she replied, smiling slightly.

"I love you, Mom."

"I love you too, baby," she replied, moving towards me and wrapping her arms around me again.

I managed not to cry somehow, but there were so many emotions running through me that I could taste sadness on my tongue. Once my mom let me go, she went to open the door to the adjacent room, and Justice and I slowly made our way through it.

"Sleep well, sweetheart," my mom said before closing the door behind us.

I was praying to do just that, and hopefully my prescription would help. "Can you give me my pill bottles out of my bag?" I asked once we'd made it to the living room.

Justice passed me my Louis bag that had been hanging from the back of the wheelchair while he went in search of something to drink. By the time I had the array of pills in my hand, he'd returned with a bottle of water for both of us. He passed me mine before using his to chase his own pills down.

"I *hate* being shot," he said, clearly frustrated, sitting in one of the two chairs that occupied the living room.

"You say that like you have a lot of experience with it."

"Some. How are you feeling?" he asked.

"Overall I guess I'm okay, but I really do want that bath, followed closely by a soft bed."

"That can be arranged," he replied, slowly rising and disappearing into the master suite. A few minutes later I hear water running, and my body was instantly calling for the soothing therapy that it offered.

"You ready?" Justice asked, coming back into the room.

"Definitely." When he wheeled me into the bedroom and then further into the bathroom I expected him to leave, but he didn't.

"Uh, I think I can take it from here," I said.

"So, you don't want me to bathe you?"

I looked back at him to gauge how serious he was, and I didn't find a hint of laughter or teasing in his eyes.

"Justice, I don't think that's a good idea."

For a second we simply looked at each other, but then he cracked a smile and backed out of the bathroom, closing the door behind him. Part of me wondered how serious he'd just been, especially since he knew my heart belonged to Rock. I couldn't yet bring myself to admit that our love had reached its conclusion, despite the fact that my earlier messages to Ivy about Rock's return had been ignored. She insisted that we needed to discuss it face to face, but that sounded too ominous for my liking. I knew I couldn't do anything about it now though, so I focused my attention on the immediate task at hand. Getting undressed was a slow process, but once I was submerged beneath the hot water and under the spell of the Jacuzzi's jets, it all became worth it. Layer by layer my stress level lowered and I was allowed to clear my mind of everything and everyone. It was short-lived because suddenly a knock came at the door.

"What, Justice?" I called out.

"I've got your towel. Is it safe to come in?"

"Yea, come in," I replied, making sure to keep everything below the neck submerged under water. I'd expected some side eye peeping at the very least, but surprisingly he only came in far enough to lay the towel on the sink and then he disappeared. Maybe my earlier comments had hurt his feelings. I didn't know, but I wasn't about to let it interrupt my moment of relaxation. I spent a leisurely hour in the tub soaking before finally bathing myself and reluctantly getting out of the tub. Since I only had one outfit, I elected to grab the complimentary robe off the back of the bathroom door, and make it my sleepwear for the night. I opened the door and came face to face with something that made me laugh.

"What the hell are you doing?" I asked, wheeling myself into the room.

"What does it look like? I'm making a pallet for me to sleep on."

"Nigga, shut up, you know damn well I'm not about to make you sleep on the floor. That bed is big enough for both of us," I replied impatiently.

I could see him open his mouth to say something, but suddenly the lights went out and I couldn't see shit. Immediately my hand sought and found the comfort of my pistol, but before I could speak, I heard a noise that explained everything. I heard gunshots, and they were close.

## Chapter 5
## Ivy

"Big!" I exclaimed, pushing off the hood of the car, running, and leaping into his outstretched arms. His 6'5", 255-pound frame swallowed my little ass, but I never felt as safe as when I was in his arms.

"Damn, it's good to see you, bae. I thought I would lose my fucking *mind* without you," he declared, squeezing me tightly.

It felt like it had been forever since we were body to body, but in this moment, I silently vowed never to be without my man again. The only way the law could have him was over my dead body.

"I missed you so much," I said, seeking and finding his mouth with my own and tonguing his ass *down*!

The way his fingers dug into my ass cheeks through my sweatpants had my pussy howling for satisfaction, making it clear to me that we needed to get the fuck out of here because we had things to do.

"I know I'm looking a hot mess, but I was expecting you to be out last night, not this morning, so - "

"You're beautiful; shut up," he said, sticking his tongue back down my throat.

It was a beautiful day around us, but he and I were quickly becoming the perfect storm and I could already feel my rain starting to drip.

"We need to go," I said breathlessly, hating to stop.

"Uh huh," he replied, moving his lips down to my neck and kissing in a way that sent electricity through my body.

"Mmm, Big, if you don't stop, we'll be fucking in front of the police station," I warned.

"Uh huh," he mumbled, gripping my ass tighter while his lips reintroduced themselves to the tops of my breasts. I could feel myself becoming weaker to the idea of resisting getting dicked down right here in front of the cops, but either of us catching an indecent exposure charge was a bad idea. I was still running all of my dad's legal businesses, and being ass naked on Snapchat wasn't a good look.

"Come on, bae, put me down," I said reluctantly. It took him a long five seconds to do so, and when he did, I could still see the passion burning in his brown eyes.

"Don't worry, we'll *definitely* finish this - but away from prying eyes. Here, you drive," I said, passing him the key to the cotton candy blue Rolls Royce I'd originally purchased for him. I'd had to have it detailed inside and out since Ebony decided to bleed all over the Italian leather, but it was still more or less brand new. I watched as he actually looked at the car because I knew he'd only had eyes for me when he walked out of the police station.

"You got a new car?" he asked, clearly impressed by what he was seeing.

"No, *you* got a new car. I had it especially ordered for you before the nightmare of you being locked up became a reality. I've just been keeping it warm for you."

"Wooooow," he replied, looking at the car and then back at me before pulling me back into his arms and kissing me thoroughly. "Thank you. I love it, bae."

"I knew you would. Now let's get out of here," I insisted, going to the passenger side of the car and getting in. Once he was behind the wheel we got on the move, putting as much space between us and the Fort Worth police department as we could while obeying the speed limit.

"Joey has been keeping me posted during his daily legal visits just like I wanted, but he didn't give me an update on Solomon. How's your dad?" he asked.

"He's as good as he can be given the circumstances. I mean, he's a long way from being himself, but I know it's in him. When I told him everything that had happened since his kidnapping, he actually told me that he respected the moves I'd made."

"I know that was huge for you," Big replied, smiling at me.

"It was. I know this isn't what he wanted for me, but it matters to me that he approves of how I segued into his world. All any girl wants is to make her daddy proud. After all, a girl's first love is her daddy."

"You still got love for me though, right?" he asked.

"Baby, that's never a question you need to ask because you have *all* my love. You're my everything."

"I hope you know that I feel the same way about you, bae. I also hope you know that I would do anything for you," he replied.

"Yeah, I know that," I said hesitantly, because I could see the devilish smile on his face. It was clear he was up to something.

"Why you sound unsure when you say that?" he asked.

"Because your ass is up to no good!"

"Oh, nah, baby, what I'm up to is *all* good," he assured me, laughing softly.

I had no idea what he had planned, but knowing him, it had everything to do with sex.

"So run down the latest," he requested.

"Well, I reached out to Ebony and offered to join forces with her, but she hasn't agreed. She just wants to know when I'm releasing Rockafella."

"So you haven't told her that Gangsta Bit has Rock?"

"I wanted to do it in person, but I don't know how to tell her or make her understand that this shit is out of my hands," I replied, feeling frustrated.

"I'll explain it to her. It'll be easier coming from me because I'm a part of this world."

"Can you explain it to me then? I mean, what the fuck is really going on with Rock and Gangsta Bit?" I asked.

"It's politics, but I suspect it also has something to do with Rock pinning that body on me. It may have been a strategy of war, but that don't mean it's acceptable to involve the law in our beef. Especially not without the superior's approval."

"So what's gonna happen to him?" My question earned me a look that told me I'd asked a dumb question. It was obvious Rockafella was gonna die, so it was really a matter of when. "Is there anything you can do to stop what's gonna happen?" I asked.

"Why would I?" he retorted, looking at me like I was growing another head.

"I don't know. It's just been a lot going on with Ebony, and she lost the baby, and...I don't know! I feel bad I guess."

"You feel bad? Forgive me for sounding harsh, but you gave up the right to *feel* when you put your big girl panties on and stepped into the family business. You gave up the right to feel when you started putting bullets into people's brains and scattering their brain matter everywhere. There is no *feeling*, babe, there are no do-overs, and there's no going back. Understand?" he asked seriously.

"Yeah, I understand. I don't see how I can mend fences with Ebony though if I can't even save her man."

"Mend fences? You're not naive enough to believe that things could *ever* go back to how they used to be. Right? I mean, I understand the guilt you feel and you wanting to at

40

least save her life, but if you think that'll somehow erase you killing her dad, you're crazy."

"Wow, you sound like Hoover Slim," I replied.

"He's telling you right, bae. Think about how much hate you had in your heart when you thought she killed your dad. The only reason your feelings have changed is because you got your dad back, but she's not gonna get that same miracle, sweetheart."

What he said made sense, even if I didn't want to hear it. All I could really do was keep my guard up and let the chips fall where they must.

"Uh, babe, what are you doing?" I asked, realizing for the first time that we weren't headed to my parents' house. We were on a familiar road though.

"You love me, right? Then just take a ride with me."

I don't know what this nigga was up to, but I knew damn well it didn't have anything to do with horseback riding. The road we were on dead ended at a piece of farm property that my family owned, and it was where Ebony and I used to ride our ponies growing up. Strangely enough, I'd found myself in this same exact location days prior. When we came to the gate that stood between us and the green grass where the cows were grazing, Big stopped the car and got out, motioning for me to follow.

"Okay, you got me out here in the middle of the sticks. Now what?" I asked.

"Now I have you all to myself, and that's what I wanted," he replied, pulling his T-shirt over his head to reveal his chest. Suddenly my mouth was dry and that pounding in between my thighs was back in full force.

"Wh-what are you doing?" I stammered, looking around, even though I knew our only audience was livestock.

He didn't answer me with words, but instead threw his shirt on the hood of the car and then unbuttoned his jeans. I wanted to ask what he was doing again, but by now it was clear. I continued watching in fascination while he pushed his jeans and boxer briefs to the ground and stepped out of them. Before me stood a man - my man, blessed by God and putting it on full display for my enjoyment.

"Amen," I whispered, biting my lip while my pussy twitched wildly.

"Your turn," he said seductively.

I wasted no time dropping my sweatpants, revealing my lack of panties, and pulling my wife beater off. All either of us was wearing was sneakers, but we were clothed in sex. In fluid motions he lifted me into the air and put me on the hood of the car while stepping in between my open legs and pushing his dick inside me swiftly. His first stroke stole my breath, but the passion of his kiss gave me new life. My legs wrapped around his back and that was all the encouragement he needed to knock my screws loose.

"I-I love you-…love you…love you!" I chanted with each pounding blow he delivered. My first orgasm came so fast that I couldn't even warn him. All I could do was scream it to the trees surrounding us.

"Oh God, babe! I missed you!" I moaned, wrapping my legs around him igniter.

"I missed you too," he growled before he bit my neck in a way that made my back arch and my pussy gush all over his dick.

I could feel him throbbing inside me, stranger than my heartbeat, and I prayed he didn't cum before I had the chance to do it again. I need not have worried because suddenly he was pushing me down until my back was on the hood of the car, and he was backing out of me, trading his pound game for his tongue skills. I felt two of his fingers dip into my wall, applying pressure on my G-spot at the same time that his tongue found my clit and flickered across it swiftly.

"Holy shit! Ohhhh! Big!" I screamed, cumming with a hurricane's force into his open mouth.

I thought he would at least give me a chance to catch my breath, but he continued the onslaught with his tongue, forcing me to wrap my legs around his head. All I could do was hold on for dear life because this nigga was talking to the pussy in a way that left me completely speechless. Aftershocks continued to roll through my body, forcing me to see stars on the back of my eyelids, and I loved every minute of it. The storm inside me was reaching new heights, and apparently Big knew that because in the blink of an eye I felt his long, thick dick once again filling me up.

"Cum inside me," I demanded, locking my legs around his waist so I could lift into his strokes.

"Baby...baby don't," he warned, gritting his teeth from the pressure I was applying with my pussy muscles.

"Cum in me," I insisted, feeling my climax peeking through the clouds of the storm we'd created.

The increased speed of his strokes told me the end was near, and as soon as I felt the first invasion of his soldiers, I let the flood gates open so we could find forever together. Long after I stopped feeling him throb inside me, we still remain joined, trying to catch our breath and get back to that place called earth.

"I-I guess you did m-miss me," I panted, smiling up at him.

"If you need more convincing, just let me know," he replied, pulling me towards him and kissing me gently this time.

"I'll definitely need more, but maybe we can take this to a bedroom."

"Anywhere you go, I'll follow," he promised, smiling.

"Let's go home then," I said, gently pushing on his chest until he backed his dick out of me. Even when it was soft you could still tell he was blessed. "Amen," I mumbled under my breath before climbing down off the car. We both put our clothes back on with the same satisfied smiles on our faces, and when we got back into the car, our hands immediately found one another.

"I knew it was somewhere private where we could be alone, and you have good memories there. I wanted to add to the collection."

"Baby, don't take this the wrong way, but when did you become so sentimental?" I asked, looking at him as if seeing him for the first time. It wasn't like Big wasn't a good man. He was a *great* man, but the thought that went into this was beyond even him.

"When you hear that door close behind you and you know it won't open again under your own power, you start to evaluate what's important in life. The most important thing in my life is you, and with whatever time we have left on this earth, I wanna create memorable moments with you. I don't wanna take a second for granted when it comes to you or us," he replied, pulling my hand to his lips and kissing it softly.

I could literally feel my heart filing with so much joy at just hearing his words, and I knew that no matter what I had to face I'd do it with him by my side.

"I'm in love with you," I said honestly.

"And I'm in love with you too. Now, always, and forever."

We made the drive to my parents' house in thirty minutes, and I don't think either of us quit smiling the whole time. I couldn't put into words how many nights I'd laid awake, terrified that I'd never have Big by my side again and wondering how I'd find the strength to go on. I was finally able to breathe a sigh of relief because I felt confident that I wouldn't have to go through life without him, and that gave me peace.

"Is that who I think it is?" he asked slowly as we pulled up in front of my parents' house. When I saw what he was looking at my smile faltered a little, coming face to face with the life I'd chosen for myself. How quickly I'd forgotten that gangsters only retired to Miami in the movies.

"Yeah, that's Ebony. And the nigga standing with her is Justice," I replied, taking a deep breath and pushing the car door open.

"They're not on the approved list, Ms. Black, but they insisted on waiting on you and - "

"It's okay, James, put your gun away," I ordered. I thought Ebony would've had something smart to say about having to wait outside at gunpoint, but one look in her eyes told me all I needed to know.

"What is it, Ebony? What's wrong?" I asked, moving to her side. The moment she locked eyes with me, I saw something in her break.

"You were right. I should've listened to you, but I didn't," she replied softly.

"What *happened*, EB?" I asked, feeling dread in the pit of my stomach.

"They attacked. They came to the hotel and shot her. My mom's dead."

# ARYANNA

WHAT BAD BITCHES DO 2

## Chapter 6
## Ebony

"Tell me what happened," Ivy requested once we were all in the house in the living room.

Just being here made my skin crawl because honestly, I wanted to be anywhere in the world except breathing the same air as this bitch. I didn't have a choice though. The reality was that Ivy was my best chance for survival *and* revenge.

"Justice and I got to the hotel at about 10 p.m. and we went to see my mom. We probably stayed with her for half an hour maybe, and then we went to the room adjacent to my mom's. I took a bath, which lasted a little more than an hour, and as soon as I came out I heard gunshots."

"Where was Justice?" Ivy asked.

"You can ask me. I'm sitting right here," Justice interjected.

"But she *didn't* ask you," Big said, his tone somewhat aggressive.

It was obvious he knew about Ivy's past with Justice, although it had come as a shock to me that my best friend had fucked around with my boyfriend back in the day. How did I not see how disloyal this bitch was all along?

"Justice was in the bedroom," I said.

"So what did you two do once the shooting started?" Ivy asked.

"Well, right before it started, the lights went out. After that, the shots happened quick, and stopped just as quick. Justice took my gun and went to check on my mom, but she... She..."

"Whoever the shooter was got in and got out within minutes, and the cameras didn't catch more than a silhouette. Somebody in the hotel was paid off more than likely, but they obviously didn't know Ebony was in the building or they would've come for us too," Justice said.

"Where were your people?" Ivy asked him.

"Back in Dallas, but they'll be getting back to town sometime today," Justice replied.

"A little late," Big commented.

"Do you got a problem, my nigga?" Justice added.

"You'll know when I got a problem," Big replied quickly.

I put my hand on Justice's to keep him from saying or doing anything stupid. Right now wasn't the time because we needed Big and Ivy, but the day would dawn when all old scores would be settled.

"What did you tell the cops?" Ivy asked, staying focused on the important topic at hand.

"A sanitized version of what I told you, and nothing about who was responsible for what happened. They offered me round the clock protection, but I turned it down," I replied.

"Smart move," Big commented.

"I'm sorry about what happened to your mom, and I know how that sounds coming from me, but - "

"Where's Rockafella? If you're truly sorry, then give him back," I said, not wanting to hear her hollow apologies. My request caused her to look at Big as if he was the deciding factor in this situation, and that made me feel more uneasy. Ivy was a creature of emotion, but Big Cuzz was one of calculation, so his decision to kill Rock would be a logical one, therefore one he probably wouldn't change.

"We don't have Rock," Big said, turning his gaze at me.

"Bullshit," Justice replied, agitated.

"You're affiliated, right? Then you understand that when you break the rules or make moves without your big homie's approval that there are consequences," Big said, addressing Justice calmly.

I was hoping that Justice would argue against what Big was saying, but he didn't.

"Where is he?" I asked.

"Gangsta Bit has him," Ivy said slowly.

Hearing this forced my stomach to lurch violently, and I thought I might throw up. Rock had told me enough about Gangsta Bit for me to know that if he felt slighted, then Rock was gonna die, if he wasn't dead already.

"Oh God, why? Why, Ivy, why would you give him to Gangsta Bit?" I asked, shaking my head as the endless sea of tears began pouring from my eyes.

"I-I didn't have a choice, EB. I *tried* to stop it," she protested.

"Yeah, I bet," I replied sarcastically. I couldn't believe the acting job she was putting on. She even turned a distressed look on Big that caused him to get up and leave the room. I could feel the hate in my body growing with each passing second, and I was preparing to launch myself out of the wheelchair at Ivy when I felt Justice squeeze my hand. Looking into his eyes helped me to center myself enough not to strangle this bitch. Barely. I couldn't look at her though because every time I did I saw everything I'd lost, everything she'd taken from me, and I hated her more.

"What's your plan for the Sinaloa Cartel?" Justice asked her.

"I-I don't know, I haven't gotten that far yet. Now that Big is out, we'll put a plan together."

"I suggest you stop wasting time, because it's only a matter of time before you become the next target," Justice warned.

"Thanks for your concern," she replied sarcastically.

"Ivy, this ain't about you and me, or Ebony and me, or *anything* that happened when we were younger. What happened, happened. If you feel like I took Ebony's side by coming down here, that's fine, but remember that only *one* of you called for my help. Even still, I didn't come out here to hurt you. I came to help solve this shit between you two," Justice said.

"All that may be true, but we both know that you *would've* hurt me for Ebony. You've done it before," Ivy retorted angrily.

Justice opened his mouth to say something, but Big chose that moment to reappear and reclaim his seat next to Ivy. I wasn't interested in whatever unresolved emotional bullshit was going on between Ivy and Justice. I was more curious about what Big was whispering into Ivy's ear. Whatever it was had something to do with me because that bitch was trying to stare a hole through my head.

"How soon?" Ivy asked Big.

"He gave us one hour," Big replied.

"If we do it, can we trust that he'll hold up his end of the bargain?" Ivy asked, looking at Big skeptically.

"Yeah, Hoover Slim will make sure of it, and he'll be there when it goes down."

"What the hell are you two talking about?" I asked, frustrated by the fact that they were talking around Justice and me.

"There's a deal on the table to get Rockafella back," Ivy said slowly.

"Do it! Whatever it is, do it," I demanded enthusiastically.

"Gangsta Bit wants six million dollars within the next hour," Big replied.

"Six million? Who the fuck he think we trying to buy back, a Kardashian?" Justice asked loudly.

"It don't matter how much he wants. I want Rock back and I'll pay it," I declared, ignoring the look Justice was giving me.

"I believe you would pay it, EB, but you can't put your hands on that kind of money that quickly, especially not with everything that's going on with your mom. You have to get her affairs in order, and that takes time," Ivy said.

"But I can't lose him too. I can't - "

"You *won't*. I'll take care of it," Ivy promised.

Immediately my eyes went to hers, looking for any signs of deception or malice on her part, but surprisingly I found something familiar. For a moment, the woman looking back at me was the girl I'd known my whole life, the girl who had my back no matter what situation we found ourselves in. I knew we could never be those girls again, but the look in her eyes made me believe she was gonna ride for me one more time.

"You'll take care of it?" I asked.

"Make the call," Ivy instructed Big.

Big pulled out his phone and went about making the arrangements, and five minutes later there was a plan of action.

"I'll wire the money offshore now. EB, I want you to take your plane, go pick up your man in L.A, and then come *straight back here*. No detours, understand?" Ivy asked, looking directly at me.

"Yea, I got it. Come on, Justice, we need to - "

"He don't need to go with you," Big said.

"It's nothing personal, Justice, but you *are* connected to Piru, so it would be like walking into the lion's den," Ivy said before Justice could say anything.

Even I knew that there was nothing he could say, but I still didn't wanna make this run by myself. I was getting ready to verbalize that when Ivy called the head of her security team into the living room to join us and informed him that he would be accompanying me. I wasn't sure how to feel in this moment. The bitchy side of me was saying that Ivy was only doing this because she had to do something to make up for all she'd done. At the same time, the side of me that knew her knew that she didn't have to do a *mu'fucking* thing, so her gestures were coming from a genuine place. I didn't know how to feel about that, so to block it out, I focused on making the arrangements for my plane to meet me at the airport here in Fort Worth.

"So what am I supposed to do?" Justice asked, obviously feeling some type of way.

"Focus on meeting up with your people and putting together some type of plan for you all to help with the war that's going on," Big advised.

I could feel Justice tense up next to me, and it was my turn to take his hand and calm him down. It wasn't that Big was wrong for what he said; it was the fact that *he* said it.

"We're gonna need all hands on deck to go up against the cartel if we want to hold them off," I said diplomatically.

"Oh, I'm not just planning to hold them off. I'm taking over," Ivy declared.

Her words turned all eyes on her, including Big's, and I could tell that her little announcement came as a surprise to everybody.

"Say what?" Big asked.

"I said I'm taking over. We're gonna push into Mexico and go after Esteban, and once he's dead, we're gonna maintain control of his empire," Ivy replied calmly.

For a minute Big just looked at her, blinking real slow without saying anything.

"Ms. Dahl, our car is out front," James said, interrupting the awkward silence. I left it to Big and Justice to tell Ivy how stupid she sounded as I allowed James to wheel me out of the house and to the black Range Rover parked out front.

"I can walk a little," I said, standing up slowly and climbing gingerly into the back of the SUV. My stomach still hurt like hell from the gunshot, but I felt stronger knowing that I was hours away from being reunited with the love of my life.

Once we were loaded up we got on the move with a truck in front of us and one behind us, which made me feel safer then I'd been in a while. I still didn't know what Ivy's motive was for doing everything that she was, but a small part of me was grateful. A *very small part*! Within forty-five minutes we arrived at the airport, and as expected, the G3 I'd inherited from my dad was fueled and waiting. Surprisingly, James and the occupants of all three Range Rovers boarded the plane with me, and every man was legally armed and prepared to kill. It became obvious to me that Ivy had always known the danger that the cartel posed to us, but my anger had prevented me from seeing it fully. That knowledge brought a certain amount of guilt with it for what had happened to my mom. My only solace in this moment was knowing that I still had Rock, and together we would have our revenge.

The flight took three hours, and I used that time to finally sleep because I was physically and mentally exhausted. The bad part about sleep sometimes is the dreams though, and I quickly found myself trapped in ones filled with my beautiful mother. I awoke just as we were preparing to land, my clothes were soaked through with sweat, and the looks on the faces around me told me that I'd probably cried out. I was too drained to be embarrassed though.

"Ms. Dahl, I received word from Ms. Black that we are not to leave the plane because the gentlemen will be brought to us. So we'll be refueling and getting back in the air shortly," James informed me from his seat across from me.

I nodded my head okay while pulling out my phone to text Justice and find out what was going on with him. Part of me knew that it was probably a good idea to keep Rock and Justice separated, but I didn't know how that was gonna be possible. How could I convince Justice that he didn't have to be by my side when that was his whole reason for coming to my rescue? One thing I knew for sure was that this whole situation had the potential to get messy, and that wouldn't help the overall goal at all. I kept my mind centered on the positive though as we landed and taxied to a hanger to standby for fuel. I couldn't stop myself from looking out of the window, wondering which way Rock would be coming from and when he would arrive. I knew I had to be careful and move slow, but I fully intended to leap into my man's arms and cover his face with kisses.

"How long do we have to wait?" I asked after ten long minutes.

"I'll check with Ms. Black," James relied, pulling out his own phone.

"Sir, There's an SUV that's stopped in front of the plane," a man said, coming to stand between James and me.

"Take four men and go out there. My orders are not to leave Ms. Dahl's side. If it's who we're supposed to meet, then you'll be escorting one man aboard, understand?" James asked.

"Yes sir," the man replied before turning and selecting the people he would take down on the tarmac with him.

I could feel the excitement coursing through my veins in anticipation of reuniting with Rock, especially after living in fear of losing him for so long. It was really him and me against the world now, but I was more than okay with that.

54

After five minutes of waiting I was getting ready to ask James what the fuck was taking so long when I looked up at a sight that stopped my heart cold. It was Rock - or at least I think it was. It was hard to tell because his face was so badly beaten that I couldn't see past the swelling into his eyes. I couldn't even tell if he was conscious because he was being carried by two men. As he got closer I saw that he was completely naked, covered in cuts and bruises, and from the looks of it, he'd been severely tortured. Sadly, the only way I was completely certain it was him was because I recognized his dick, even though it was swollen from obvious kicks.

"Oh God, babe, what did they do to you?" I whispered in horror.

"Eb-Ebony? Is that y-you?" he mumbled through swollen lips.

"It's me, babe, you're safe. You're safe now," I promised.

# ARYANNA

## Chapter 7
## Ivy

"We need to talk," Big said.

"I know. Meet me in my dad's office, I need to talk to Justice real quick," I replied, giving Big a look I hoped he'd understand. The air needed clearing and I was gonna do that right now. Thankfully Big took the hint and left Justice and I alone I the living room.

"I'm not sure what your play is, but shit is about to get thick around these parts so you might want to clear out," I advised.

"You seem to be forgetting that I'm not here under *your* invite, and it's obvious that Ebony still wants me here."

"*Wanted* you here, as in the past tense. She's got her man back now, and he'll do the protecting from this point on," I said, smirking.

"Oh, so *that's* why you paid six million, just to get me out of the way? I didn't know I still meant that much to you."

"You don't mean shit to me. As far as I'm concerned, you're just another body that can take a bullet for my cause. I'm simply trying to keep the bullshit to a minimum because Ebony is going through enough right now," I replied honestly.

"You don't give a fuck about *what* Ebony is going through, especially considering that you're the cause of her greatest pain."

His words stung because in part they were true. I was woman enough to admit that I'd made some mistakes, but I still cared about Ebony. I didn't have to prove that to anyone except her though.

"You can think what you want, Justice, but my position on you being here remains the same. Shit's about to get heavy, and none of us got time for you to be stepping on your dick. I don't want you and she don't need you, so if that's why you're here, you can go back to Cali. Dying for stupidity's sake seems beneath you, but it's your choice. Show him out," I said to one of the security guys in the room as I stood up and headed for my dad's office. I wasn't being overly confident about my ability to handle the Sinaloa cartel without help, but I felt like help from Justice would be more of a hindrance than an asset. There was simply too much at stake to gamble on him, especially with Rock back in the picture.

"Sorry, bae, I needed to handle that," I said, coming into the office and closing the door.

"What's this takeover shit you're talking about?" Big asked immediately.

"It's crossed my mind before, but today's events really brought it home for me. I mean, let's be real, these mu'fuckas ain't gonna never stop coming, and I'm not giving up *nothing* that we own, so it's winner take all."

"You must be punch drunk if you think it'll be that easy. You think the Sinaloa cartel is the only cartel in Mexico, or that the other cartels will let your black ass run shit south of the border? Come on, bae, really? You're black, you're an American, *and* you're a woman! You're tripping," he replied, shaking his head.

I could tell that this was about to turn into a heated argument, and that's not what I needed at the moment. I didn't respond to what he said right away, but instead I made my way behind my dad's desk and took a seat. The look on his face told me he was waiting on me to respond, but I was waiting on him to sit down so we could discuss this in a civilized manner. Finally, after two long minutes, he took a seat.

"So tell me what you suggest, Big? We keep going back and forth exchanging bullets? How many of your homies are you willing to lose to this ongoing war? How much money are you willing to lose? You've gotta look at this from the big picture, babe."

"No, *you* have to look at the bigger picture! You could *die* trying to pull some shit like this off - or has that slipped your mind?" he asked hostilely.

"You're right, I could die, but how is that any different from every day of the rest of my life? As much as it hurts me, my dad ain't getting up out of that bed, and that means it's on me to make sure his life's work doesn't get taken from him. *I'm* what's standing between him and the wolves, and you want me to go at this half-assed? Is that how you would play it?"

I knew he opened his mouth to continue arguing, but my last question was starting to sink in. He was way better versed in warfare than I was, but what I was saying made logical sense, which made it hard to argue with.

"So what's your plan, Ivy?"

"I haven't gotten that far, Big, but that's what I got you for. Right?" I asked, giving him my most seductive smile.

"Stop looking at me like that. You know it makes my dick hard," he said, fighting not to smile.

"I knew how to handle your hard dick, bae, but I need your help to pull this off."

"You already know I got you, that's not even a question you need to ask. What about the Gulf Cartel? Have you run your plan of action past them yet?" he asked.

"No, I need to talk to my dad first."

"I suggest you go do that now because it's obvious that we're about to be under attack."

I knew he was right, but truthfully, I was a little nervous. Before when I had been making decisions it had been in his absence, but now I was getting ready to bring an idea to him that he had every right to veto. If he did that, I didn't know what my next plan of action would be.

"I'll go see him after I wash the scent of you off me," I said, getting up.

"Don't worry, I'll get you all dirty again later."

"Why wait? You need to shower too," I replied, taking his hand and pulling him along with me.

In anticipation of his release I'd bought him some clothes, since his were either at my house or his house in Houston, and I'd laid everything out on my bed.

"Damn, babe, you didn't have to get me a new wardrobe. And what's with the suits?" he asked, looking at the bed covered with business wear and casual business wear.

"I understand you're a street nigga, and I'm not trying to change you, but you're also my man and that means when we step out, you represent me. I represent tens of millions of dollars in legal business, which means I can't run around in sweatpants and wife beaters, no matter how comfortable they are. That also means jeans and T-shirts won't work for you, but I did get everything big enough for you to be able to conceal your guns on you."

"Well thank you for that, at least," he replied, sarcastically.

"Aww, baby, don't be angry with me. I only did this because I need you by my side always, no matter if it's in the trenches or in the boardroom," I said, taking his hand again and pulling him towards my bathroom.

Once I had him behind closed doors, he wasn't worried about what I wanted him to wear because I was standing in front of him wearing only my smile. He immediately followed suit, and suddenly what should've been a quick shower turned into forty-five minutes of me climbing the walls while he had his way with me. It was times like this that I was grateful my dad was on the first floor because I was a slave to my man's dick, and I wasn't shy about voicing it. After getting dressed, it was still another twenty minutes before I made it down to my dad's room because I made sure to suck the aforementioned dick until my man was speaking in tongues. I had to show him how much he was truly missed.

"There you are. What took you so long to come see me?" my dad asked as soon as I came through the door.

"It's been a *long* morning, Dad, and I'm sorry I'm just now coming to see you."

"It's okay. You're here now, so tell me what's going on."

"Well, for starters, Joey finally got Big released on bail this morning," I said, taking a seat next to his bed.

"That's good. Did you have to put up everything?"

"I had to put up both houses and two restaurants, but Daddy, you know Big would never do anything to make us lose anything," I said confidently.

"I know that, sweetheart, otherwise I would've told you not to do it. That's obviously the good news of the day, so go ahead and tell me the rest."

I ran down what had happened to Marissa and about Ebony showing up here. I almost lost my nerve when it came time to tell him what I thought our best move should be, but I pushed ahead and laid it out for him. I also told him how Big felt about what I wanted to do, just to have all opinions out in the open. When I finished talking I waited in silence while I watched him process all the information I'd just given him. My dad's body wasn't the same, but the intellect was clear to see in his eyes, and that meant his mind was still the well-oiled machine it had always been. That gave me comfort.

"Do you believe your plan of action is the right one?" he asked.

"Yes I do."

"And what about the Gulf Cartel? How do you see them reacting?" he asked.

"I think they'll lend their full support because all they care about is their bottom line. We make great money together, even with me having to send the dope to the East and West coasts right now, and it's only gonna get better when the dust settles."

"I think you're right about everything you said so far, but something Big told you can't be ignored. There's no way they're gonna let some black, American, woman come into their country and run a mu'fucking thing. They'd betray you the first chance they get, and not just another cartel or up and coming faction, but the Gulf Cartel as well. That's *their* world, sweetheart, and there's no outsiders aloud. *Ever*. Now, what you can do is convince the Gulf Cartel to align themselves with you and the Hoovers, promising them that when the dust settles you will be their exclusive export resource for any and all contraband. They get to expand their territory, which gives them a firmer grip on all illegal activities in Mexico, and our problem goes away. Plus we make more money," he concluded.

Now it was my turn to digest what was being said. Somehow hearing it from my dad was different than hearing it from Big, but it wasn't because I didn't trust Big's opinion. Big's first reaction to anything was to protect me, even if it was from myself. My dad seemed to understand that I could take care of myself, which allowed him to focus on giving me the soundest advice for whatever situation I was facing. It was clear to me that my dad had come to accept my role, and so he would make me the best at it. Every decision was life and death.

"You're right, Dad, as always," I replied.

"Not always, sweetheart. I just have the benefit of being in this game longer than you have, so I've seen more, that's all. I do want to tell you this, and listen closely because I mean every word. *Watch everybody.* I don't give a fuck who it is, and that includes Big. You watch every mu'fucka around you or in your circle. We all play this game on borrowed time, and sometimes we forget that the closest knife that could stab you in the back is the one right next to you. I didn't see it coming and that's why shit is the way it is. Watch everybody," he said vehemently.

Part of me wanted to tell him that he was being extreme by including Big's name in his warning, but how could I say that knowing he was lying here because of decisions his best friend made?

"I understand, Daddy, and I will keep my eyes open, I promise."

"Don't just keep them open. You gotta learn to grow eyes on the back of your head. What I mean is that you have to learn to read people and their motivations to anticipate their movements. Study their ambitions as close as you would their weaknesses because they're equally important," he said.

My dad and I had always had open lines of communication with each other my whole life, but the jewels he was dropping on me right now were those once in a lifetime lessons you only got at the foot of greatness. I felt honored to be his daughter.

"I understand," I repeated, taking his hand in my own. I knew he didn't feel it, but he saw it and it made him smile.

"Good. Now go handle business, but be back in here by lunch time because I wanna share a meal with you," he demanded.

"Yes sir," I replied, leaning in to give him a kiss on the cheek before making my way out of the room.

I went straight to my dad's office, where I found Big waiting on me. For a moment I had to pause and stare at him leaning against the desk, looking F-I-N-E in his dark blue suit, white shirt, and baby blue tie, with matching Gators on.

"Damn, you clean up nice," I admitted, feeling my pussy twitch in agreement.

"I know. You did a good job picking out the clothing though because this black billionaire fits like it's tailored."

"You're welcome. And now it's time for your sexy ass to go to work, I said, retaking my sear behind the desk and pulling out my phone.

"What did your dad say?"

"He said that we go to war. Ready the troops, because it's on."

## Chapter 8
## Ebony
## 2 weeks later

"I brought you a cup of coffee, sweetie, just how you like it," Nurse Valerie said, handing me the cup.

"Thanks Val," I replied, accepting the much-needed caffeine while suppressing a yawn. I couldn't remember the last good night's sleep I'd had because I refused to leave the hospital, but the nursing staff had taken care of me almost as well as they had Rock. Even thought I'd been through the pressure and stress of late night cram sessions and final exams, these sleepless nights were the longest fourteen I'd ever endured. From the moment Rock was carried onto the plane I knew I was literally watching his life slip away. My first instinct was to get him to the nearest hospital, but Ivy and her team had insisted that I get him back to Fort Worth, where we'd both be protected. As much as I hated her, I hated and distrusted the people who'd done the damage to my man more, so I'd brought him here. It was a miracle that we both made it in one piece, considering the fact that I'd cried hysterically for the whole three hour flight.

"How is he doing today?" Val asked, sitting beside me on the loveseat that was a few feet away from his bed.

"He's doing better, the doctors say. The swelling to his brain is almost completely gone, and the doctor said there shouldn't be any permanent damage from the first week he spent in a coma. Still no word on when he'll be released though."

"That's not something you wanna rush, baby. You want him to be completely healed before he steps back out into the world," Val insisted.

"I know you're right, but it *kills* me to see him laying in that bed," I confessed, fighting back the tears that always wanted to bust free. Rockafella was larger than life and always had been, so to see him like this broke my heart into a million pieces. I loved him no matter what, but I wanted the old Rock back, I wanted to feel safe again in his arms.

"I understand, but you have to be thankful he's *alive*, especially after the ordeal he went through," she replied optimistically.

I knew she was right about that because it had been worse than what it looked like on the plane. When we found out about the brain swelling that led to him slipping into a coma almost immediately after arriving at the hospital, we also learned of his internal injuries. He'd had four ribs broken, but luckily none of them punctured his lungs. His right knee and been shattered too, and that required surgery to have a titanium replacement put in. Once the swelling in his face went down, more discovered were made, which included the loss of his left eye and the partial severing of his tongue. Luckily the doctors were able to piece his tongue back together, and it was healing nicely, but his eye was a different story. They couldn't repair what they didn't have, so Rock would forever have to wear an eye patch. All in all, yeah, he was lucky to be alive.

"I'm thankful to still have him. He's all I've got," I said softly.

"What happened to that handsome young man I saw hanging around you for the first few days after you arrived?" she asked.

"He went back home. There was nothing for him to do here, and he just kept trying to convince me to go home."

"It's okay to take a break every now and then, sweetie. I'm sure your man would understand," she replied soothingly.

"He would understand, but he needs me and I need him, and there's nothing more important than that in this world right now," I said definitely.

I'd known Justice meant well by suggesting I get out of the hospital for a while, but he should have remembered how stubborn and determined I was. I appreciated his help - all his help - but my complete focus had to be on Rock now.

"Well, I know your man appreciates your sacrifice and your love. And if he doesn't, he'll just have to answer to me," she replied, smiling and standing up.

Out of all the nurses that worked here, Val was my favorite because she reminded me of my late grandmother. She always had a gentle smile and kind words, but there was a strength about her that anyone could easily recognize.

"Let me know if you need anything," she said, turning towards the door.

"Actually, there's one thing I do need. Does this hospital keep a priest on call?" I asked.

"I'm sure they do. Why do you ask?" she replied, clearly curious.

"I just need to have a word with him, if possible."

"I'll see to it," she promised, leaving me alone with Rock.

I took a healthy drink of the still-warm coffee, needing it to wake me up and help organize my thoughts. I really wanted to know what progress Ivy was making when it came to our common enemy, but that wasn't a conversation we could have on the phone, and I didn't want her coming here. Rock had been *absolutely furious* when I told him that I was actually working with the bitch, but he'd calmed down when I explained everything that had happened. He understood the logic, and begrudgingly agreed with the position I'd taken, but that hadn't softened the hate in his heart, and I didn't blame him. The downside was that all I knew about Ivy's actions was that based on the local news reports, she'd obviously gone on the offensive. There were bodies dropping all over Texas and only a small percentage black or belonging to the Gulf Cartel. There had been car bombs, shootings, kidnappings that led to entire families being massacred. I had to give it to Ivy: the bitch wasn't playing *no games*. I wanted more though. For all I'd lost, I wanted my hands soaked with the blood of my enemies. I wanted that as badly as I did for Rock to make a full recovery <u>ASAP!</u> Pulling out my phone, I sent Ivy a text saying that I was just checking in with her. Hopefully she was smart enough to know what I really meant, because exchanging pleasantries wasn't what I was after.

"Hey babe," Rock said weakly, snapping my focus away from my phone and putting it squarely on him.

"Heyyy," I replied, quickly moving to the chair I kept beside his bed and taking his left hand. "How are you feeling? Do you need anything?" I asked.

"No, I'm good. I've got you," he replied, smiling slightly.

"You'll *always* have me, baby, you should know that by now."

When he squeezed my hand, I felt my heart rate quicken with both love and hope. He was getting stronger. I could feel it.

"I need some sleep," he said.

"Is that your way of saying that I'm looking a hot-ass mess?" I asked with mock irritation.

"Never that. It's my way of saying that I love you and I'm glad you're here, but I know you haven't left my side."

"Why would I? Where would I go? Everything that matters to me is in this room," I replied seriously.

"Did you go to your mom's funeral?"

I closed my eyes briefly, remembering the only time I'd ventured away from Rock's side, and the pain that came with it. I'd halfway expected Ivy to shoot up the service like I'd done her mom's, but she didn't. She actually showed up to pay her respects to a woman she once loved as much as I'd loved her mom, and surprisingly, her actions made me feel a little guilty. Even though I'd been unable to cry on her shoulder, I couldn't deny that there was a part of me that looked across my mother's closed casket at Ivy and took comfort. It was a tough moment for both of us.

"Yeah, I went to the funeral. Ivy put together a nice service," I conceded.

"Ivy put it together? Why?

"Because I couldn't. Not just because I've been here with you around the clock, but because I couldn't bring myself to do it," I said sadly.

He squeezed my hand again in comfort and I felt my love for him swell. Suddenly my phone vibrated with a response from Ivy that left my mouth dry.

"What is it, babe?" Rock asked, obviously sensing that something serious was going on.

"It's-it's Ivy. She says that she has my mom's surprise guest, and she's asking if I want to meet him."

"Is she saying what I think she is?" he asked slowly.

"Yeah. She has the mu'fucka who killed my mom."

It felt so good to say those words, but I knew it would feel even better to see whoever it was suffer and die. The question was could I leave Rock to witness it.

"Where is she?" Rock asked.

"I don't know, and she probably won't say in a text message."

"So what are you gonna do?" he asked simply.

I knew if I turned the question back around on him and asked what I *should* do, he would say that it was my decision. After everything that happened, there was no way I could be scared of this moment, plus I felt like I owed it to my mom. With my decision made, I sent Ivy a simple text back telling her to come get me.

"I should only be gone for a little while, baby, I promise," I said, reclaiming his hand.

"It's okay, babe, I'll be good. Plus it gives me a chance to fart because I be holding it when you're in the room," he replied, laughing softly.

"Eww! I know your ass is gonna stink! I still love you though, and as soon as I get back I'm gonna prove it."

"I wish you could, but my dick is still too sore to do anything except piss," he replied sadly.

"That's not the only way to prove my love, sweetheart. I got something special planned."

"Oh yeah, like wh-"

"Ebony, that favor you asked for is out here in the hallway," Val said, poking her head in the door.

"I'll be right back, babe," I said, giving his hand a quick squeeze before following her out into the hallway.

The priest was a tall black man with an easy smile and kind brown eyes. "My name is Thomas Bishop, what can I do for you today, young lady?"

I shook the hand he offered and explained what I needed from him, making sure to put emphasis on the fact that I wanted it done as soon as humanly possible. Part of me thought that he might object, but his eyes twinkled with delight instead.

"It'll take a day or two, but it can be done," he assured me.

"Thank you Mr. Bishop. I'll be stepping out briefly, but you'll be able to find me here day or night." We shook hands again before I went back into Rock's room. As soon as I sat down my phone went off again with a text from Ivy saying that she was sending James to get me, and I should be out front in five minutes.

"Baby, I'll be back as soon as I can, okay?"

"Woman, I know that. Just go handle it and get some piece of closure," he replied.

I leaned over to kiss him softly, feeling the heat reverberate from my head to my toes at just the feel of his tongue dancing with mine. Even though I knew I shouldn't, my hand still found its way beneath his hospital gown on an adventure in search of eggplant.

"While I'm gone I need you to talk to the doctor about when I'll get to use this again," I whispered against his lips.

"God I hope it's soon," he mumbled, wrapping his arm around me and pulling me closer.

If I had time I would've said fuck the doctor's advice, opinion, *and* orders, but I had to meet my ride out front.

"I'll be back soon," I said, kissing him one more time before standing up straight.

"Be careful, and *don't* turn your back on that bitch," he warned.

There was no need to ask who he meant because we both knew.

"Don't worry, I won't," I replied, heading for the door. By the time I made it downstairs in the elevator, James was out front in a Range Rover waiting on me along with two other Range Rovers.

"What room is Rock in? Ms. Black has specified that from now on he stays guarded at all times," James said.

"He's in room 502," I replied, climbing into the back of the SUV James was in.

After dispatching some of his men into the hospital, we got on the move. I wanted to ask where we were going, partially because I was curious, but mainly because I was paranoid enough to know that Ivy could be trying to eliminate me. This whole thing could be an elaborate ruse to separate me from Rock so she could kill us both. It was a chance I was willing to take though, and not because I trusted her in the slightest, but because in my heart of hearts, I was giving her the benefit of the doubt. My initial thought was that we'd be leaving Fort Worth, but the scenery remained familiar and it became increasingly more familiar until I knew where we were going.

"She would pick this spot," I said aloud.

"What was that?" James asked.

"Nothing, just talking to myself."

It was still another thirty minutes before we arrived at our destination, pulling up behind the cotton candy blue Phantom that Ivy had been driving recently. When I stepped out of the truck I spotted Ivy and Big standing in the middle of the field where we used to ride our ponies and play for hours when we were kids. I started walking in their direction, expecting James and his men to follow, but instead the Range Rovers reversed the way we'd come until they disappeared from sight. It wasn't until I got a few feet from Ivy and Big that I saw the prone figure of a man laying at their feet, bleeding on the wildflowers. Now I knew why the hired help had left. The only good witness was a dead one.

"Glad you could join us on this sunny afternoon," Ivy said, smiling.

"I'm here. Who's this?" I asked, nodding at the naked, bleeding man. It was clear that he'd been given one *vicious* ass whooping before he ended up in the position he was right now, but the rise and fall of his upper body indicated that he was still alive.

"This is Esteban's favorite nephew, his most trusted sicario. This is the man he sent into the Marriot in Houston to kill your mom, so this is the first man to answer for that. But not the last," she replied, handing me a gun.

# ARYANNA

## Chapter 9
### Ivy

I could tell by the look in her eyes that she wasn't expecting what I was offering her. She'd come out here to witness justice being served - justice for the mother she'd lost - but I knew it would mean more if she took this man's life. It wouldn't lessen the pain of losing her mom, but it would be something to hold onto when she thought the pain was unbearable. I wished I had something like that to console me at night. I would explain all of the things to her if she needed prompting or motivation, but I wouldn't divulge my selfish reasons for giving her this opportunity. We were at war, and everyone had to pull an equal amount of weight. You couldn't fight for someone who wouldn't fight for themselves, so it was important that everybody put their own work in at some point. I needed to make sure Ebony understood that concept, and I also needed to be certain she couldn't betray me without swift and costly consequences.

"Take it, EB," I said, offering her the Glock .40 again. I didn't see fear in her eyes, but there was a little bit of uncertainty swimming within the hazel as she took the gun from my hand.

"How do you know it's him?" she asked skeptically.

"Ask him yourself," Big replied, kicking the man viciously just to make him scream.

"Did you kill my mom?" Ebony asked, becoming more choked up with emotion with each passing second.

"It was my uncle's orders. I had to - "

The rest of his excuse was lost in the thunder of rapid fire gunshots until all you heard was the clicking of the empty gun in Ebony's hand. Her hand had been steady while she was pulling the trigger, but now I noticed a pronounced shaking as all the emotions she felt came rushing to the surface. Despite our differences, I felt for her, and in the end, I'd loved her mother too.

"Come here," I said, taking the gun from her hand and passing it to Big while pulling her into my arms.

I'd expected some type of resistance, but she came to me willingly enough, laying her head on my shoulder and crying her eyes out. I did my best to soothe her without words, just holding her and stroking her hair the way I'd done her whole life when times got unbearably tough. Big, sensing that we needed a moment, started towards the car and left us alone. There was so much I wanted to say, and even more that I wanted to apologize for, but part of me knew that speaking wouldn't help. Ebony didn't need my words, only my support. For a full ten minutes she continued to weep, until finally she was under control enough to step back and look me in the eyes.

"Th-thank you," she stammered, wiping her nose with the back of her hand.

The girl standing in front of me was a shell of the one I used to know. Ebony Dahl didn't wear jeans and stained white T-shirts, or keep her hair in a ponytail constantly, not even on her down time. She was too high maintenance even for that. Yet somehow here she stood before me, looking broken, and I felt guilty about that.

"You don't gotta thank me. You might've done the same for me," I replied.

"No, I wouldn't have. What happened to us, Ivy? How the fuck did we *get* here?" she asked, looking around at what used to be our field of dreams.

"Sometimes I ask myself that same question. It seems like those college girls, those bad bitches who were to slay the University of Texas campus, are complete strangers now – and not just to each other. I wonder who I *really* am when I look in the mirror," I confessed.

"I don't look in the mirror. There's too much pain there."

"Listen, I know it's probably not worth a whole lot, but I'm *truly* sorry. There's a lot of shit I wish I could take back, shit that I'll never be able to make up for. I'm determined to try though because I refuse to watch you die at the hands of some bean eating mu'fuckas," I said sincerely.

"I'm supposed to trust you?" she asked, taking a step back.

I tried not to be offended by her actions or her tone, but it was hard work. I felt like somehow she forgot that her dad was the one who set *all* these events in motion, but I knew that reminding her would only increase the distance between us.

"I'm not asking you to trust me because that's not realistic. I'm in this with you though, and that's a reality you can hold onto. No matter what happens, I'm in this until Sinaloa goes back to being nothing more than a town in Mexico. They're out to erase our very existence, *and* everything our families worked for, but you can trust that I'm not about to give them shit except bullets," I replied sincerely. Staring into her eyes, I could tell that her heart was beating right now with the thrill of revenge, and that she liked it. We not only had a common enemy; we had common ground to stand on, and that could potentially help to bridge the gap between us. Baby steps had to be taken first.

"I've been paying attention to the news. Is that you?" she asked.

"Nah, that's us! I'm not out here doing shit just for personal gain, EB, I'm making moves with you in mind. The Gulf Cartel is behind us one hundred percent. Shit, they actually fronted me a metric ton of coke when I bought the last one! Not to mention that the Hoovers are seeing so much money that any one of them would cut their own mother's throat if I asked them to."

"How close are you to actually getting Esteban though?" she asked, unimpressed by my business savvy.

"He's holed up in his compound in Mexico, but I'm working on a plan to get in. You wanna help?" I offered.

"My place is with Rock right now. That's what is important to me."

"I believe you…but I also see that thirst for revenge in your eyes. Don't lie to yourself. You want it as bad as I do," I replied confidently.

"That may be true, but Rock is my *first* priority."

The conviction in her tone was clear, which put us at an impasse on this topic. Still, I felt like progress was made overall.

"I understand, and I'll keep you informed if you want," I offered.

"That's fine."

"Good. Now that this little matter is settled, we need to go because you have more business to handle," I said.

"What business? I need to get back to the hospital, and that's all I'm focused on right now."

"I promise I'm not trying to keep you from the hospital, but you need to sit down with my lawyer. I had him take care of everything involving your mom's estate, and there's paperwork for you to sign. Plus, no offense, bitch, but you look a hot-ass mess right now and that's completely unacceptable," I said.

"Okay, for *one*, I ain't your bitch and these ain't the old days where your opinion mattered to me. For two, why would I trust your lawyer? You think I'ma sign my mother's money over to you so you can take that like you did my father's?" she asked angrily.

I had to check my anger before I responded with some real hostile shit, followed by a punch to her damn face. It was obvious that she wasn't giving more than an inch at a time.

"You can take the paperwork to any lawyer of your choosing before you sign it. I only had Joey do the legwork for you because I understood you would be preoccupied with Rock. As for me wanting you to get your shit together physically, don't you think it would help Rock to know that you're doing okay mentally? He *knows* you, EB, so when you come in looking like a cat left out in the rain, he knows that you're struggling. That adds stress on him, and I know that you don't want that. All I'm suggesting is that you take care of yourself because it'll make it easier to take care of him," I stated calmly.

The fight in her eyes was still there, but it didn't hide the fact that she knew that I was telling the truth. It may have been hard to accept coming from me, but that didn't make it any less true.

"Where's your lawyer?" she asked, sighing in defeat.

"At the house. Come on," I said, leading her away from the man she'd killed. We walked to the car in silence, but it wasn't an awkward silence, so I was grateful.

"You got this?" I asked Big once we'd made it to the car.

"Yep, my people are on the way," he replied, handing me the key to the car.

"Good. I'll meet you back at the house," I said, giving him a quick kiss before moving to the driver's side door. Ebony followed my lead, and we got on the move. After twenty minutes of silence, I finally worked up the never to push the envelope one more time.

"So, you're gonna shower and change at the house, right?" I asked.

"Yes, bitch, damn! If it'll get you off my ass, yes!"

Her response made me laugh, which eventually made her laugh, and before long we were hysterical and in tears laughing. Neither of us questioned why; it just felt good to laugh instead of cry. It took us an hour to get back to my parents' house, but by the time we did, I felt like something had healed between us, even if it was only a little something.

"You know where my room is and you definitely know your way around my closet. Handle your business," I said once we'd got into the house.

"I won't be long, so have your lawyer ready with the paperwork so I can get back to Rock."

"I got you," I replied, heading towards my dad's office. For the first time I actually felt like with enough time, Ebony and I might get some part of our old relationship back, and that made me smile. It wasn't gonna make me let my guard down, but it did make me smile.

"Sorry to keep you waiting, Joey," I said, breezing through the door.

"It's okay. I've just been sitting here nursing my second glass of your dad's eighty-year-old scotch. Don't worry, I peeked in on him and got his permission first."

"Smart man. Ebony is upstairs taking a quick shower, but she'll be down shortly. I told her about the paperwork, and because she doesn't trust me, she's gonna want to take it to her lawyer," I said, pouring myself a drink from the decanter sitting on the desk and taking a seat.

"That's her choice, but I assure you, everything is in order and above reproach."

"I have no doubts, it's just that things are still difficult between us, and there's no trust."

"I never thought I'd witness the day when you two would be at odds like this," he replied, shaking his head sadly.

"Yeah, I know, I said softly, tipping my glass and taking a healthy swallow. Times were certainly more different now than I ever would've predicted them to be, but that was life, and all anyone could do was make adjustments.

"So, how are the businesses doing?" I asked, changing subjects.

"Thriving, which is never a bad thing. I got a call from a prosecutor friend of mine and it turns out that the witness against Big is having some credibility issues, *and* possible availability issues. It's not official yet, but I have a feeling that the collateral you had to put up will be turned back over to you soon."

This news made me smile because it seemed like Hoover Slim was a man of his word, and I liked that.

"Keep me informed, because when it's all over, I'm taking Big on a much needed vacation to - "

The sound of my phone going off interrupted our conversation, but once I saw who was calling, I had to answer.

"What's up, Jeremy?"

"We've got a problem," he replied quickly.

I signaled for Joey to excuse himself because I didn't want to risk his plausible deniability by having him listen in on this particular conversation.

"What is it?" I asked once I was alone.

"Two shipments got hit in the last forty-eight hours, and it wasn't by law enforcement."

"Where, and who?" I asked simply.

"On the West coast, and we don't know who because it was done at sea. Professional job though."

"The cargo?" I asked.

"Both ways."

His response meant that we got hit for drugs *and* electronics, which meant the loss in dollars wasn't something

I wanted to hear. Unfortunately for me I was the power behind the throne so I didn't get to stick my head in the sand.

"The cost?" I asked reluctantly.

"More than two million."

Someone had *clearly* come up on a nice payday courtesy of me, and hearing that soured the good mood that I'd been in. My father had warned me that losses were to be expected, but not ignored. You had to find the problem and fix it because that was working smarter and not harder.

"Change everything - schedules, routes, ports, all of it - and do it quickly," I ordered.

"I figured you'd say that, and the necessary changes are underway as we speak. Will you be notifying your people out west?"

"Yeah, I'll take care of it. Make sure to put *everyone* on your staff on high alert because piracy outside of international waters is rare, which makes me believe we're deliberately being targeted," I said, frustrated that I didn't anticipate this move from the cartel.

"I'm on it, and I'll be in touch."

After disconnecting the call I tossed back the rest of my drink, and quickly poured another to replace it. In my anger I wanted to guzzle my second drink too, but instead I sipped it slow while thinking of what my next move should be.

"Wow, I see you've picked up a new bad habit," Ebony said, coming through the door, followed by Joey.

The difference in her appearance was like night and day, but it didn't hold as much interest for me as it had earlier.

"Joey, give her the paperwork so I can take her back to the hospital," I said, taking another sip from my glass.

My lawyer did as instructed and retrieved the papers from his briefcase, passing them to Ebony. She took a seat opposite from me and looked the documents over for a few minutes before looking up to meet my gaze.

"This shit is all legit, right?" she asked.

"Yeah, it is, but take it to your lawyer and let them look it over. It won't hurt my feelings," I assured her.

For a few moments she just stared at me, and then she picked up a pen off the desk and put her signature on every page that required it.

"Can you make sure everything is filed properly, and I receive a copy once it's done?" she asked Joey, holding the papers out to him.

"Of course I will. I'll get on top of that right now," he replied, grabbing his briefcase and leaving the room.

"You want one?" I asked, gesturing towards the liquor bottle on the desk.

"That's probably not a good idea, even though if *anybody* needs one, it would be me."

"You ain't never lied. If you're ready to go, I'll take you back, and don't worry, this is only my second drink," I said, tossing the fiery liquid down my throat.

"Actually, I wanna talk to you about something first."

Hearing this statement from her had my curiosity piqued, to say the least.

"I'll bite. What's on your mind?' I asked.

"You told me earlier that you were doing this for *us*, right?"

"I did say that, and I meant it," I replied sincerely.

"Then I want you to do something. I wanna go after Gangsta Bit. That shit he did to Rock *can't* go unanswered, not when I have to look at him in pain every single day."

I don't know what I expected her to say or ask, but somehow this request hadn't crossed my mind. It probably should've though because she loved her man as much as I did mine, and if them niggas would have done Big like that, I would've gutted their mamas in front of them. This wasn't an easy thing to do for her though because killing Gangsta Bit compromised my relationship with Hoover Slim.

"You wanna kill Gangsta Bit, huh? Honestly, EB, that's something I gotta talk to Big about because - "

"We both know if you take it to Big, he'll talk you out of it because it could be bad for whatever arrangement Global Gangsta has with the Hoovers. This is a call you've gotta make on your own, and you have to use your cartel connections to make sure it gets done properly - that is, if you're serious about trying to make up for some of the shit that's happened."

It was on the tip of my tongue to ask her if giving up six million dollars wasn't enough to prove that I wanted to make shit right, but I bit back those words. I knew she was right about what would happen if I took this to Big, but I still felt some type of way about keeping shit from him. What it all came down to was one question: did I owe her this? Staring into her eyes, I knew the answer without question.

"I got you, EB."

## Chapter 10
## Ebony
## 2 days later

"By the powers vested in me, I now pronounce you husband and wife. Go on and kiss your bride, son," Thomas Bishop said, smiling at Rock and me.

When my husband opened his arms, I melted into his embrace, kissing him from the very depths of my soul while tears of happiness slid from my eyes. It was a relief to be crying for a good reason for a change, and an even bigger relief to have made it to see my wedding day. It wasn't exactly how I pictured it, but the most important thing was that I'd gotten to marry the man that I loved more than life. Originally I'd thought it was gonna be difficult convincing Rock to go along with a ceremony in his hospital room with only nurse Valerie as our witness, but he'd surprised me. Not only was he with the whole idea, but he'd even insisted on standing up at the foot of his bed so we could hold hands and look each other in the eye. It was perfect.

"I love you, wife."

"And I love you too, husband," I replied, smiling up at him.

"You two look so happy together, and I'm honored that you let me be a part of this moment. Now get back in bed," Val ordered, going from wedding guest back to charge nurse in the blink of an eye.

"What about our first dance?" Rock asked, not releasing me or moving towards the bed.

"That knee is too new for dancing. Now off your feet," Val said sternly.

"We'll dance, don't worry," I whispered, smiling. While Val helped him back to bed, I shook hands with the priest and thanked him again for doing this for us on such short notice. He congratulated us and then left, and thankfully Val followed his lead because I wanted nothing more than to be alone with my husband.

"You look amazing in that dress," Rock said, smiling at me.

"You like it? I swiped it from Ivy's closet," I replied, looking down at the partially sheer white Givenchy dress that was hugging all my curves.

"Can you breathe in it though?" he asked, laughing.

"Oh, I can do more than that in it. Just hold on," I replied seductively.

I grabbed the chair that I kept by his bed and wedged it under the door so no one could get in before I quickly climbed into the bed with him.

"Babe, the doctor said - "

"I don't care what he said. It's our wedding day and we're gonna consummate this marriage right here. Right now," I said, reaching beneath his hospital gown and gently taking his dick in my hand.

Any words or objections he had were lost in the moans that were coming from deep in his throat, and I knew that I had him lost. My hand motions were soft, yet deliberate, as I brought him to life quicker than an Indian snake charmer. Once he was hard enough to bend steel, I climbed on top of him and slowly took him inside me a little at a time.

"This dress is g-good for easy ac-access," I said, going up and down as slow as I possibly could.

"Take it off," he demanded hoarsely, grabbing at the fabric and pushing it over my hips.

I pulled it the rest of the way over my head, leaving me wearing nothing except my white stilettos. The feeling of his hands becoming reacquainted with the landscape of my body had my heart ready to leap out of my chest and my pussy throbbing with equal intensity.

"I m-missed you. I missed *this*," I moaned, trying not to move too fast. I didn't want to hurt him, but the feeling of him touching every wall inside me was like God giving me *life*, and I wanted to embrace it with every breath I took.

"I love-love you," he panted.

"I love you m-more, my husband," I replied passionately, moving faster under the steady guidance of his hands on my hips. I pushed his hospital gown all the way up to his neck so I could lay down on his chest and feel his heated flesh pressed firmly against my own. His hands found my ass, palming both cheeks and forcing me down on his dick faster and harder.

"B-baby," I breathed into his mouth, worried that I was pushing him to do too much too soon. He didn't loosen his grip though, and I honestly couldn't have stopped bouncing on his dick if I wanted to.

"Ohhh fuck, fuck yeah," I stammered, cumming in a wild rush that had me bucking uncontrollably.

Rock held on tight though, slowing down his strokes enough to thoroughly rattle my entire body with my orgasm. It felt like a tsunami in between my legs, but the steady pounding of my man's dick was proof that he knew how to swim. Suddenly I heard noise coming from behind me and I knew someone was trying to get in the room.

"Eb-Ebony?" Val called out.

"Hold on, Val," I yelled, sitting straight up on top of Rock and putting my hands on his chest while taking us to the next level.

"We gotta make this q-quick," I said, taking the training wheels off and riding him like I was being chased by the boogie man. When his eyes rolled to the back of his head I got nervous, but his grip didn't loosen, and I didn't slow down.

"Ebony, open the door," Val called out.

I ignored her words because I was seeing the most beautiful sunrise on the back of my eyelids, and the Promised Land was near.

"B-babe, I'm cumming," I warned, pumping my hips faster while digging my nails into his chest.

"Me too," he replied right before I felt his cum explode into me. That immediately triggered my own climax and I came as quietly as I could so whoever was outside the door wouldn't hear me. As badly as I wanted to stay on top of him with all of him inside me, I knew I had to open the door.

"Now you're officially my husband," I said, kissing him and hopping up in search of the dress I'd tossed to the floor.

"If that's all it took, we've been married for years now."

"Ha-ha, smartass," I replied, slipping the dress on and making myself presentable before going to the door.

"Pull your gown down," I whispered fiercely, shaking my head. Once he was covered, I moved the chair and opened the door.

"Sorry, Val," I said sheepishly, smoothing my hair down.

"It's okay, I just - whoa! Been a long time since I smelled *that* smell," she said, giving me a knowing look and a devilish smile.

I knew I was probably red in the face with embarrassment, but I had to have it, and when she left I planned on getting some more.

"I just came to give you two some more good news because you've officially been discharged," Val said, smiling at Rock.

"For real?" I asked excitedly.

"I wouldn't lie to you, sweetie. You can take your man home and celebrate your wedding day properly," she insisted.

"Baby, stop asking questions and get the car," Rock demanded, already sitting up in bed, grinning like a fool.

"Just be careful with him," Val whispered to me, giving me a wink before she backed out of the room.

"Oh, your ass is in trouble *now*," I said, smiling mischievously.

"That's what you think. Pass me that bag in there so I can get dressed and we can get the fuck out of here. I need a bubble bath."

I did like he asked because I couldn't have agreed with him more. It was time to go. After taking my gun out of my Louis V bag, I tucked it into my purse and passed him the bag.

"You need help?" I asked.

"I think you've done enough for now," he replied, wincing slightly with his movements.

I wanted to feel bad, but my pussy was too satisfied for me to feel anything other than utter joy. While he was getting dressed, I sent Ivy a text and let her know that Rock was being released and we'd be going to the nearest hotel for the rest of the day and night. After that, I ordered us a limo so we could make our exit in style.

"Okay, our ride should be here in about twenty minutes, so I'm gonna go and make sure your paperwork is in order because we don't need *any* delays," I said, heading out the door.

I found Valerie at the nurse's station and we talked for a while, waiting on the discharge paperwork to be processed into the hospital's system. Once that was done, I gave her a hug and thanked her for all of her help during this extremely difficult time. When I got back to the room, Rock was already dressed, sitting in a wheelchair with the now-empty Louis Vuitton bag and my purse in his lap.

"Ready, willing, and able," he said, smiling at me.

"I bet you are. So, do you wanna go straight to a hotel or do you wanna go out to eat somewhere?" I asked, getting behind his wheelchair and pushing him out of the room.

"I just want to go to a hotel. We can always order room service if we get hungry."

"What do you mean *if* we get hungry? I don't know about you, but I damn sure just worked up an appetite back there in that room, and you gonna have to feed me before the next round," I replied seriously.

"Yes ma'am. Any other demands?"

"Love me forever, or I'ma kill you my damn self," I promised, wheeling us onto the elevator.

"That ain't *never* something you gotta worry about, babe. I'm yours for life and I'm gonna do my best to live a *long* life with you."

My heart swelled at his declarations because I wanted nothing more than forever with this man, but my mind thought about the threats that still existed for both of us. I hadn't yet talked to Rock about my request for Ivy to kill Gangsta Bit, or that Ivy agreed to do it. I wasn't sure how he would react, not because he didn't want revenge for what had been done to him, but because I knew deep down he had a healthy fear of Gangsta Bit. Fear was a hell of a motivator.

"I hope you don't think we're gonna be living in a hotel for long because once we come back from our honeymoon, we're picking out a house," I said, pushing the wheelchair out of the elevator towards the front door.

"I'm fine with that, but where are we going on our honeymoon?"

"I don't know yet. We'll decide that together. All I know is I wanna be gone within the next seventy-two hours," I said, already picturing sandy beaches and nonalcoholic fruity drinks. As we got closer to the door, I saw the black Mercedes limo sitting right at the curb with the driver leaning against it, waiting patiently. It was a beautiful Texas spring day and the afternoon sun felt good on my skin.

"I think we should enjoy the day before we - "

The rest of my sentence was frozen in my throat because the afternoon sunlight took on a brighter shine when the light reflected off of the gun barrels aimed in our direction. I had time to tip Rock over from the wheelchair to the ground before the perfect spring day suddenly came alive with a thunderstorm of gunfire.

"Stay down!" I yelled, scrambling for the gun in my purse.

The shots were coming from the left and the right, effectively pinning us down and rocking the car shielding us like a baby's crib in a tornado. I was too afraid to stick my head out and take aim, so I just fired wildly in both directions. Sooner than I liked I heard the dry clicking of my empty gun, and I knew our problems had just got worse because I didn't have any extra mags. I was just about to wonder where the fuck Ivy's people were when I heard what sounded like two SUV's sliding to a stop on the other side of the limo. Looking at Rock, I could tell we were thinking the same thing. We were hoping it was the cavalry, but it could just as easily have been whoever was trying to kill us.

"Get in the car!" I heard a familiar voice yell.

I quickly opened the back door of the limo and helped Rock in first, and that's when I caught sight of James standing in the street, holding court with an AR-15. I had no idea where the limo driver was, but as soon as I'd thrown myself into the back with Rock, the car pulled off fast. The ride wasn't luxury, but I was just thankful it got us the hell out of there in one piece.

"You okay?" I asked Rock, helping him up onto the backseat.

"I'm fine." His words didn't match his tone because it was clear that he was *homicide* mad! I lowered the partition to tell the driver where to take us, but I saw that there was one of James's men riding shotgun, which meant we were going to Ivy's house. Sure enough, thirty minutes later we pulled up to Ivy's parents' house, where she and Big were standing out front.

"Baby, listen to me, I know you don't wanna be here, but you know like I do that there's nowhere safer for us right now," I said, taking his hand.

"From the looks of shit, them two right there are the least of our problems. I don't like being here, but I like being dead even less, so I'll deal with it."

I kissed him, more grateful for his presence than anything I'd ever been given in life. It hurt my heart to know that I'd almost lost him again, but it made one decision about my future crystal clear. Ivy and I had to join forces. I opened the door and climbed out, passing Ivy my empty gun so I could help Rock out of the car. I knew he was in pain, but he damn sure wouldn't show it in front of these two, and I didn't blame him.

"What happened?" Ivy asked once we were all standing in the driveway.

"They tried to hit us once we came out of the hospital. Where were your men?" I asked.

"I texted you and told you they were on the way. You should've waited," Ivy replied.

I had some hot shit on my tongue to spit at her, but I realized that I hadn't checked to see if she messaged me back, and right now I had no idea *where* my phone was. This wasn't the time for fighting anyway.

"It takes a lot of balls for a broad daylight hit. You must've pissed them off," I said.

"The cartel is a formidable opponent, and - "
"It wasn't the cartel," Rock said confidently.
"How do you know that?" Big asked.
I looked at Rock myself, wanting the answer.
"Because the shooters were black."

# ARYANNA

# Chapter 11
# Ivy

It wasn't impossible that Esteban had hired some locals to take out Rock and Ebony, but so far the war had been waged with him using his people. You couldn't trust just anybody with a murder-for-hire situation because this was 2018 and a mu'fucka would fold quicker than a bad poker hand. Even though I was new to this, I still didn't see Esteban going from a known entity like his nephew to just some random niggas on the street. But just because I couldn't see it don't mean it wasn't happening.

"I think it's best for you two to stay here for now, at least until we figure out who Esteban is using," I said.

"*If* it's the Sinaloa Cartel at all," Rock chimed in.

"Do you know something you're not sharing with the rest of us?" Big asked.

"No, I just know Gangsta Bit is a snake-ass nigga, and I wouldn't put it past him to take the money you all gave him and *still* try to dead me," Rock replied.

None of us offered up a rebuttal or any type of argument because we all knew that what he said could be completely accurate. It was in no way good news considering that we already had one more than formidable opponent to deal with.

"Big and I will check that angle, but either way, everyone is safer here," I said, locking eyes with Ebony so she'd understand that I still intended to do what I promised her.

"If we're in the crosshairs of more than one organization, then *nowhere* is safe. All we need is an escort to the airport and we're out of the country on our honeymoon tonight," Rock said.

"Honeymoon?" Big and I replied in unison.

I looked at Ebony's ring finger and sure enough, there was a diamond on it big enough to choke a rabbit.

"Y-you got married?" I asked, surprisingly hurt that she would do something like that without me there.

For the moment our feud was forgotten, and I was feeling some type of way that the girl I'd considered my best friend for the better part of my life had stepped into womanhood without me there to witness it.

"Yeah, we actually did it about an hour ago," Ebony replied, blushing slightly.

"Oh. Well, congratulations," I said, forcing a smile on my face.

"Thank you," Rock replied.

"I don't think it's a good idea to leave the country. I respect that you took your vows and everything, but being in a foreign country without protection is more dangerous than staying here. I know it's a new concept to you Rock, but you gotta start thinking like a neutral nigga," Big said.

Following his statement the two men simply stared at each other, communicating without words and leaving Ebony and I oblivious to their conversation.

"You mind if I take a bath? It's been awhile," Rock said finally.

"EB, help him in the house and get him settled. You two can take my room," I said.

"Thanks," she mumbled, taking Rock's hand and moving slowly with him into the house.

Once they were out of sight, James joined me and Big.

"What did you see?" I asked.

"At least four shooters, all black, but not wearing anything to identify them as part of any street gang. I suspect we'll know more sooner than later because two of them didn't make it, and that little demonstration is sure to be on every local news station within an hour," he replied.

"Okay. Make sure security is tight, because we're gonna hold up here until further notice," I said.

"Yes ma'am."

I waited until he'd walked away before turning to look up at Big.

"What do you think, babe?" I asked.

"Rock could be right, or it could be the cartel figuring some locals would be easier to disguise, making it easier to get to them."

"This is Texas, babe. There are damn near the same amount of Mexicans as Blacks, so the cartel didn't have to go the route of using unknown shooters to blend in," I replied thoughtfully.

"So what do you think?"

"I'm not sure who it is, but we need to keep our eyes in every direction because we don't need any surprises," I said.

"True. I'm gonna reach out to Hoover Slim and see what he knows," Big replied, kissing me on the forehead before heading back into the house.

I took a few moments to myself so I could organize my thoughts and figure out what my next move would be. It had to be calculated because if we *were* fighting multiple enemies, I needed to be able to anticipate their moves as best as I could. If Rock's thoughts about Global Gangsta were true, then my first move was clear. Going back into the house, I went straight to my dad's office and opened the safe to retrieve my secure cell phone. I made sure the door was closed and locked so I wouldn't be interrupted before dialing the number I had in mind.

"Manuel, I have a proposition for you," I said, hoping I was making the right move. Our conversation lasted a brief ten minutes, ending with the leader of the Gulf Cartel agreeing to what I needed done for the small fee of $1.5 million. If I would've thought of this sooner, I could've saved myself $4.5 million of the $6 million I'd recently paid out! Once I was off the phone I sat down in front of the computer and transferred the funds immediately. With that piece of business complete, I knew it was time to go see my dad and update him. I just hoped he'd be okay with my most recent plan of action.

"Hey, Daddy, how you feeling?" I asked, walking into his room and sitting by his bed side.

"I'm fine, sweetheart, what's up?"

"Nothing much, I just wanted to check on you and make sure you didn't need anything," I replied.

"Uh huh. You checked on me not too long ago, and since you've never been able to lie to me, why don't you just tell me why you're here, sweetheart?" he said, smiling.

I had to smile too because no one knew me better in this world than he did, not even Big. No one's opinion mattered to me more either.

"Well for starters, Ebony and her husband are upstairs in my old room right now," I said hesitantly.

"Oh, this should be good," he replied, wide-eyed.

I proceeded to tell him about the most recent shooting and the various opinions about who could be behind the attack. Then I had to let him know about the move I made against Gangsta Bit.

"Did you talk things over with Big before you gave the assignment to the Gulf Cartel?" he asked

"No, because if I did, he probably would've told me not to do it."

"And he might've been right, sweetheart. Let's be clear about one thing first: you don't owe Ebony a *goddamn* thing, not nothing, understand? You're allowing yourself to be controlled by your emotions when it comes to her, and that will get you killed. You can't *ever* lose sight of the fact that I'm laying here in this bed because of what her father did, and your reaction to the entire situation was the right one. I understand that the Sinaloa Cartel played out family and her family against each other, but *none* of that would've been possible without Jacob's betrayal. You don't owe her *shit*, got it?" he stated passionately.

"I got it, Daddy," I replied, feeling completely chastised and put in my place.

"Good. Now I know better than anyone that you can't unring the bell on your move against Gangsta Bit, and it might *not* have been a bad move in overall scheme of things. On the one hand it threatens whatever peace or agreement Big has with Global Gangsta, but at the same time, Gangsta Bit sounds too reckless and unpredictable to turn your back on. Killing him now could save you a lot of hassle later, and you did it without getting your hands dirty, so it shouldn't come back to you. The only problem really is that Ebony knows too much."

"I've got an angle to keep her in line, don't worry," I said confidently.

My statement earned me a raised eyebrow, which forced me to explain the backup plan I'd put into play to counter any bullshit from Ebony.

"Taking a page from their book, huh? Fair exchange ain't never been robbery, but even with that backup plan, I still want you to keep your eyes on her," he instructed.

"I plan to do just that, which is one of the reasons I insisted that they stay here. I'm keeping my enemies closer."

"Good girl. What's your next move?" he asked.

"I think I need to - "

I was interrupted by my phone ringing, and it was Jeremy's ringtone. "What now?" I said, under my breath, pulling the phone out of my pants pocket. "Please don't have more bad news for me," I said as soon as I answered.

"I'm afraid so. We need to meet ASAP."

"Where are you?" I asked, sighing.

"Myself, Louis, and Roger will be at the port in Laredo in a couple hours. Can you meet us there?"

"I'm on my way," I replied, hanging up.

"What's wrong?" my dad asked.

"I don't know. Jeremy and the Jones brothers wanna meet at the Laredo port, and all I know is that it's not good news," I said, frustrated.

"Whatever it is you can handle it. Just take your time."

"I will. I love you, Daddy, and I'll see you when I get back," I replied, giving him a quick kiss before heading for the door.

"Take Big with you, and be sure to tell him everything," he called after me.

That wasn't a conversation I was looking forward to having, but I knew my dad was right about it being necessary to have. I should've never kept shit from Big *anyway*, and now I had to hope that he didn't flip the fuck out on me. Bracing myself, I went in search of my partner in crime and found him in the kitchen with the refrigerator door open, drinking from the gallon jug of orange juice.

"You a sucka nigga for that," I said, laughing.

"And you love me, so deal with it. I assume you just came from speaking with the old man, so what did he have to say about our house guests?"

"I'll tell you about it in the car. We've got somewhere to be," I said seriously.

"Uh oh, that don't sound good."

I didn't comment on his speculation. Instead, I turned around and headed out front to the car.

"James, I've gotta go out for a while, but I'm taking Big with me so you can just send one SUV of people with us," I said, catching him coming up the front steps as I was descending.

"Not a problem, Ms. Black. I'll go with you and - "

"No, I want you to personally watch over the security here. Choose your best men to accompany us. I trust your judgement."

"Right away, ma'am," he replied, disappearing into the house.

"You ain't in the car yet?" Big asked, coming up behind me and smacking me on the ass.

"Don't start nothing that I can't finish right now," I warned, going to the driver side of his car and getting in.

"You know, I'm starting to think that you bought this car for yourself and not me because you drive it more than I do."

"I'm only driving because I know where we're going, but you can drive home if it makes you feel better," I replied.

"Tell me where we're going," he said, getting in the car.

"To the Laredo port for an emergency meeting, and before you ask, I don't know what the meeting is about or why I've been summoned to it. There's something more important I have to discuss with you though. I made a move against Gangsta Bit," I blurted out.

Big looked at me for a long thirty seconds, blinking real slow before speaking.

"Explain what you mean when you say you *made a move* against Gangsta Bit."

"You know what I mean. That's not the type of nigga you go at halfway. It needed to be done though," I replied defensively.

ARYANNA

"Ivy, we don't even know that Gangsta Bit was behind the shooting today, so why move against him, and why do it without talking to me?"

"I didn't do it because of today's incident, I did it because I promised Ebony I would. She asked me to do it because of what happened to Rock, and I felt like I owed her that."

"You felt like you owed her that," he repeated slowly.

"You don't even have to go there. I already got that lecture from my dad."

"Oh, well maybe he'll get through to you about the dangers of emotion in this game because you *obviously* ain't hearing me!" he said heatedly.

"Babe, it's not like that. You *know* I value your opinion. I'm sorry, I made a mistake by keeping this move from you."

"You made a mistake by thinking that killing Gangsta Bit was the right move right now! We're already in the middle of one war and you somehow saw it as smart to start another one? Don't get too drunk on your newfound power, sweetheart, because it's gonna get us *both* killed," he replied, his brown eyes alive with his anger now.

"Big, give me some credit. I made sure that whatever happens to Gangsta Bit won't come back to us. A nigga like him has too many enemies to pin his disappearance and death on one person without hard evidence. And at the end of the day, it needed to be done because I'm sure he saw weakness in me for paying so much for what he perceived as a disloyal mu'fucka."

My logic kept his mouth shut for the moment, but the anger was still blazing in his eyes. I caught sight of men coming out of the house and climbing into the Range Rover parked behind us, forcing me to start the car and get on the road. An hour into the drive, the car was still bubbling with a tension-filled silence, but I wasn't about to be the one to break it. I'd fucked up, so I had to wait for his anger to run its course. In the meantime, I was focused on what the fuck could've happened that would require the top people in my illegal business partnership to call an unscheduled meeting. It was mandatory that we all got together once a month to discuss our enterprise, but this meeting here was a deviation from the norm.

"No more secrets, Ivy, and I mean that shit," Big said finally.

"Agreed," I replied readily, glad to be past the storm of disagreeing with my better half.

For the rest of the drive we discussed the pros and cons of the move I'd made and how we'd handle any questions from Hoover Slim. One thing we both agreed on was that no matter what happened, we weren't telling Hoover Slim that I was behind anything that happened. That truth wouldn't do us any good. By the time we reached the port an hour and a half later, I felt like Big and I were on the same page again, and I vowed to never jeopardize that for anyone or anything.

"I'll wait here for you," Big said once I stopped the car in front of the office my dad kept here for business.

"No, you're coming in with me. Whatever the problem is, I want your opinion on what the solution should be," I said sincerely, getting out of the car.

He didn't argue, but instead followed my lead into the building.

"Okay, what's the emergency - "

I didn't get to finish my question because one look at Jeremy's face told me that shit had gotten real for him recently. His hair was as disheveled as his appearance, and the closed black eye behind his glasses looked nasty *and* painful.

"Wow," I whispered, taking a seat across the table from the other three men in the room.

"This is nothing. I can handle this. What I can't handle is the fact that he has my child, my eighteen-year-old son, and he won't give him back unless I become his man at the ports of his choosing. Just meeting with you right now could get my son killed, but I need your help, Ivy," Jeremy said, fighting back tears.

"Of course I'll help you, and I'm so sorry this is happening to you and your family," I replied, feeling his pain personally because of what I'd gone through with my father being taken from me.

"Who did this?" Big asked.

In response to Big's question Jeremy pulled out his phone, and after finding something on it, he slid the phone across the table to us. I couldn't believe what I saw.

"That *motherfucker*!"

## Chapter 12
## Ebony

"Your sponge baths are *way* better than those nurses at the hospital, babe," Rock said dreamily while I soaped up his chest. "Ow!" he exclaimed, jumping from the shock of having his nipple twisted.

"Don't play with me, nigga, because you know *none* of them bitches gave you a bath while I was there, and if I find out you pulled some shit when I was gone, I'ma beat your ass," I warned.

"I was only joking, babe. You know I don't want no one else touching me except you."

"That's what I thought. All jokes aside though, how are you feeling?" I asked, resuming my thorough washing of him from my seat behind him in the tub.

"Physically I'm okay. Being in this house though..."

"I know what you're saying, but it's a means to an end and that's all. I didn't agree to stay here just because it's safe. I actually have something I need to tell you."

"What is it, babe?" he asked, looking up at me.

"Ivy and I had a conversation the day I took care of that business involving my mom's killer. I told her wanted Gangsta Bit's head for what he'd done to you."

"Big won't agree to that, and even if he did, he'd have to get approval from Hoover Slim, which won't happen," Rock replied.

"I figured out some of that, which was why I told her not to take it to Big and simply handle it on her own to show me she was serious about fixing shit. She agreed to do it."

"And you believe her?" he asked skeptically.

"Yeah, I do. I think she's going after him, especially given what happened to us today and your theory on it. I saw the look on her face when you were talking out front, and I'm telling you, she's gonna make a move on him sooner than later," I stated confidently.

"She better know what she's doing, because that nigga ain't nothing to fuck with."

We both were living in the truth of that statement right now. It had been hard for Rock to talk about, but he'd told me bits and pieces about what was done to him, and the conclusion I'd drawn was that Gangsta Bit had wanted him to beg for death. I'd thought the worst injuries were the visible ones, but he'd experienced something that I wouldn't have wished on anyone. Maybe not even Ivy.

"So, how do you feel about her going after Gangsta Bit?" he asked suddenly.

"I love it. It was my idea, remember?"

"That's not what I mean. Ivy is making this move solely because you asked her to, not because it's strategic or good for business. She's doing it with the hopes of getting her sister back. How does that make you *feel*?" he asked again.

His question was a valid one, but not really one I knew how to answer. I knew that things could never be the same for me and Ivy, but somehow they weren't as bad as they'd been just a few weeks ago. I tried not to think about it so I wouldn't have to explain it, or feel like I was betraying my dad by feeling anything other than raw hatred for her. But now my husband was asking the tough questions, and I couldn't lie to him. I couldn't give him the unvarnished truth either because I knew he still blamed Ivy for his suffering at the hands of a man he once considered family.

"Honestly, babe, I don't know how I feel because I'm not worried about her. My motivations are purely selfish at this point," I said.

"I get that, but we both know that this bitch is playing some type of angle, even if it's only to get back in your good graces. That would only allow her next betrayal of you to be that much easier, and we can't let that happen. We don't need friends. All we need is each other."

"I couldn't agree more," I replied, kissing his neck softly.

I loved this man beyond reason and I'd do anything in the world for him, including risk the bite of a snake. What he didn't know wouldn't hurt him as far as how close Ivy and I got.

"Sit on the edge of the tub," he demanded, turning over in the water to face me. At first I didn't understand what he was up to, but with me sitting like he wanted, he was suddenly face to face with his favorite thing to eat. "Now put your legs on my shoulders and lean back," he instructed.

I did exactly as I was told, watching with building ecstasy as he gave new meaning to the saying, "Look, Ma, no hands". His slow licks started from the ground floor, and by the time he made it to my clit, I felt like I was dangling off a roof, and I was *losing* it.

"T-taste good, don't it?" I said, grabbing his head.

"Mmm hmm."

The feeling of his teeth on my clit sent electricity through my body, and he quickly followed that up by sucking on it like it was his favorite Slurpee. I felt like he was playing three card monte with his bites, sucking, and sticking his tongue deep in my pussy, but he knew what he was doing because I came for him within minutes. Before I knew it, he had one of my legs hooked in his arm which did allow me to literally hang upside down from the tub while he devoured me.

"Rock! D-don't let go! Oh shit! So g-good!" I moaned passionately.

This time when my orgasm hit, I thought I might blackout, but I rode the wave like I'd seen heroin junkies do on TV until I finally stopped shaking.

"We've *gotta* add that to the routine," I said, struggling to sit upright.

"We'll pick out the tub for our new house together," he replied, smiling, oblivious to the new shine my pussy juices had left on his face. There was no way I wasn't gonna satisfy him, so I slid back into the tub and rode his dick until he literally bit a hole in his lip. At that point I thought we should stop, but it was another thirty minutes of bloody kisses and passionate fuck faces before he was satisfied enough to un-join us.

"Seems like your dick ain't as sore as it was because you're back trying to damage the kitty," I said, climbing out of the water and grabbing a towel.

"What can I say, babe? Your kitty has healing powers," he retorted, laughing and following my lead. We both headed into Ivy's walk-in closet naked, where I grabbed some shorts and a t-shirt, and Rock found one of Big's old sweat suits to throw on.

"What do yo wanna do now?" he asked.

"Nigga, I told you that you had to *feed me*! Did you think I was playing? Come on here," I said, taking his hand and pulling him behind me.

I knew he wasn't comfortable in this house, but a bitch wasn't about to starve!

"What do you want to eat?" I asked once we'd gotten to the kitchen.

"I don't care; you choose," he replied, side-eyeing all the security people walking around.

"Well, I'm in the mood for some fried chicken, so while I'm getting all the stuff I need, why don't you turn on the TV over there/"

"Don't they have a cook or something?" He asked.

"Did my mom have a cook? She may have had someone to clean the house but if you stepped foot in her kitchen, that was your *entire* ass. Ivy's mom was the same way."

"That trait didn't rub off on you, did it?"

"I don't know. Now that I'm a wife, I could see me cooking family meals for us and - "

It had been on the tip of my tongue to speak about our baby as if he or she was still growing inside me, instead of in heaven with my parents. There was no way to forget the pain of that loss, nor was there a way to stop yearning for it all to have been a horrible dream.

"Hey, it happened for us once and it'll happen again, baby. You *will* be a mom," he said confidently, coming up behind me and wrapping his arms around me tight.

I could feel the love in his embrace, and even though it didn't stop the pain, it did give me hope.

"You making promises like that, you better be ready with that dick," I replied, grinding on him.

"I'd do it right here, right now if we didn't have an audience," he replied, licking my earlobe slowly.

He gave me the shivers in the best possible way, but I wasn't comfortable fucking all over *this* particular house.

"We'll get back to that as soon as I have something in my stomach besides you. Now go sit down and watch me work," I said.

Rock reclaimed his seat at the kitchen counter after turning on the TV and he kept me company while I made us lunch. Despite all the things that had gone wrong to put us in this exact situation, being here with him in this moment felt right.

I couldn't count how many times I'd seen my parents share time and space like this, laughing and joking while sharing something so simple as good food and conversation. It was my hope that they were looking down on us, proud that we'd be carrying on this tradition.

"How many pieces of chicken do you want?" I asked.

"Do I get any sides with that?"

"Uh, I think there might be some French fries in the freezer that I can drop in some hot grease for you," I replied.

"That'll work, and I'm good with two breasts," he said, smiling suggestively.

"You would say that with your nasty - "

Suddenly his smiling face became a fading background that I saw in my peripheral because my attention was drawn to the face on the TV screen. The news program was interrupting regularly scheduled programs to talk about a shooting that I was all too familiar with, and they had side by side pictures of the two shooting victims. In all the chaos, I hadn't got a good look at any of the mu'fuckas who'd been trying to put us in the ground, but now that I did, I definitely recognized one of them.

"It was only a matter of time before that came to light. You know that, babe. I'd rather it was their faces than ours though," he said after following my eyes to the TV screen.

It was clear that he thought my rapt attention and sudden speechlessness were by products of the shooting being made public, and I know now wasn't the time to tell him different. Rock was *far* from being one hundred percent, and if I told him what I knew, he'd be unstoppable whit it came to going after our enemy. I hated keeping shit from him, but this was for his own good.

"At least they haven't gotten ahold of the footage from outside the hospital yet, because that'll definitely show me shooting back," I said, refocusing my attention on cooking. "It was self-defense. That'll be clear no matter *what* angle they see it from."

He was probably right, but I was still trying to make sense out of everything I knew. Knowing the shooter meant I knew who sent him, but that conclusion brought me more confusion than clarity. I needed to find some answers, and sadly, I knew there was only one person to get them from. I finished up making our lunch and we sat down to eat, making sure to avoid talking about the attempt on our lives anymore. Instead, we focused the conversation on life after the drama because we both had a lot to look forward to. Rock and I both had thought that an exit from gang life would leave him feeling incomplete since that was what he'd known for so long, but we were realizing how wrong we'd been. He was free of any excuse for bullshit to intrude on his life for the first time in forever, and that put a world of possibilities at his feet. I'd been bitter about Ivy taking over our father's illegal empire, but those feelings were quickly fading because all I really wanted in the world was the love my husband could provide. Materially, we had everything we could ever need, so all we had to do was survive this moment and the world was ours. It sounded easy, but I knew it wouldn't be.

"Okay, babe, it's time for you to go upstairs and rest," I said, clearing our dishes from the table.

"Why do you say that like you ain't coming with me?"

"Because I need to get in front of this shooting situation, so I'ma get with Ivy, and I know you don't want to be there," I replied convincingly.

"You're right about that. Don't take long though. Technically, this *is* the beginning of our honeymoon."

"I won't be long. Hold on, babe, I'll help you back upstairs," I said, coming from around the kitchen counter. Once I had him relaxed in Ivy's bedroom, I grabbed my phone and purse and went in search of Ivy.

"James, do you know where - "

"Ms. Black and Mr. Big had an unscheduled appointment, and I don't know when either of them will return," he said curtly.

"Oookay, well, let her know that I'll be back soon. And I don't need any of your people to go with me," I replied, walking past him and heading for the garage.

Just like I'd hoped, I found Ivy's silver Aston Martin waiting for me, with the keys on the peg board by the door. I hopped in, but I made a call and sent a text before firing the engine and pulling off. My mind was racing with countless questions because the obvious truth was simply too hard for me to believe. After everything I'd been through, one would think I'd know that people's betrayal and treachery don't come with boundaries, but in this case, I had to hold out hope until I had a face to face with this enemy. It took a half hour to get to the airport, but I was in the air a short fifteen minutes later because my plane had been ready and waiting for me. An hour into my flight, I finally got a response to my text message, and now I had a meeting scheduled to take place at the Four Seasons hotel as soon as I could get there. My next order of business was to make sure that I had a car and driver to meet me on the tarmac. In the back of my mind I knew that I was taking a huge risk by walking into this situation alone and unarmed, but I didn't really see any other way to do it. For the rest of my flight and the car ride to the hotel, I questioned the decisions that had brought me to this point, wondering if I'd done the right thing by taking this trip without telling anyone. If I was wrong, I could easily disappear from the face of the Earth, and no one would know why or who'd done it. The problem was that I didn't know why I was targeted for death before arriving here, and I needed the answer to that question.

"Wait here," I instructed the driver.

After taking a couple deep breaths, I stepped from the car and walked into the hotel, going straight to the elevator because I knew the room number. A few minutes later the door to room 505 was opened and I was admitted without question.

"I'm surprised to see you in L.A. To what do I owe the pleasure?" he asked.

"I came to find out why you're trying to kill me, Justice."

# ARYANNA

## Chapter 13
## Ivy

"When did you get this picture?" I asked, fighting to regain my calm because uncontrollable rage was threatening to take over.

"I get one every day, as a reminder of what will be taken from me. It's only been forty-eight hours, but my son looks worse with each photo. What am I supposed to do, Ivy?" Jeremy asked emotionally.

I couldn't take my eyes away from the photo of Jeremy's son Harley standing side by side with Justice, wearing a terrified expression as his face. I'd known Harley and his mom Kristen as long as I had Jeremy, and they were all good people undeserving of this kind of hell, despite Jeremy's duplicitous occupation. For it to be somebody from my past, someone I considered an acquaintance, if not a friend, to inflict this harm made me feel nauseous with guilt. It was clear that Justice had lost his goddamn mind, so I had to figure out a way to rescue Harley without provoking him. One thing I'd learned from my previous experience was not to be hotheaded or pull the trigger too fast, but before it was all over, Justice would pay for his treason.

"What exactly does he want you to do?" I asked, finally looking Jeremy in the eye.

"Any shipment of yours that he can't hijack he wants lost in the stacks and rerouted to a port he'll choose. He's promised to let my son go after five successful shipment takeovers, but only because he'll be overseeing everything personally from inside the Port Authority system, so he'll have proof of me breaking the law. He's not gonna stop until he's taken what you have," Jeremy replied.

"We can't let this happen, Ivy. It puts all of us at risk for exposure," Louis said.

"Who is he, Ivy?" Roger asked.

"An old friend," I replied tightly.

"Will he kill my son?" Jeremy asked, looking at me with his heart in his eyes.

"I won't let him," I replied confidently.

"So what's your plan? Because going at him sideways could end badly," Louis said.

"You're right, it could. What Justice is obviously hoping for is to take advantage of my current entanglement with the Sinaloa Cartel and take over everything because I'm distracted or dead. The only advantage we have right now is that he doesn't know I'm on to his play, and we need to keep that advantage. The only way to do that is to give him what he wants," I replied.

"What?" Big asked, speaking for the first time and looking at me like I was growing two heads. "Ivy, you can't - "

"Everyone just *listen*. If I go at Justice and his people with guns blazing, Jeremy's son dies, period. We need to buy time, and the only way to do that is to make him think he's getting what he wants."

"And how do we do that?" Big asked.

"We make the next two shipments easy to steal, and we spread them out over three weeks. He's targeting our West coast operations, so we're gonna have to stop pushing big product by water and start trucking it in. That way we don't lose our clientele. There will still be a loss of money, but I'll eat that since I'm responsible for him being anywhere near our operation. If we still need more time, then we'll have to move shipments to the ports he wants," I replied.

"What do you plan to do with the time you're buying?" Louis asked.

"The less you know, the better," I replied cryptically.

"How's this plan gonna get my son back? He said that he wants at least five shipments," Jeremy said worriedly.

"He'll get five, but only two will be dope. Moving drugs leaves less of a footprint than electronics, which means he's about to bite off more than he can chew. What we're gonna do is reach out to our black market connections and make sure they only buy directly from us. We'll even lower the prices if necessary. The bottom line is that Justice ain't about to come up like he thinks he is, and I'm getting your son back alive. Tell Kristen that," I said, staring directly at Jeremy.

"Are you sure about this, Ivy?" Roger asked.

"I am. Just trust me."

The three men looked at each other briefly, and when their eyes landed back on me I didn't see doubt in any pair.

"What's my next move?" Jeremy asked.

"You make contact and tell him that another shipment will be in the water next week, and I'll make sure it is. You and I need to maintain daily communication, and I want updates if anything significant happens. I'll also need to know the moment that your son is safely returned because I'm not making a move until then. Louis, Roger, I think now would be a good time for a family vacation, preferably somewhere out of the country. You don't make it seem suspicious, just spontaneous, and make sure you two stay in contact with me too. We won't schedule anymore face to face meetings for the immediate future, but if it becomes absolutely necessary, I'll send Big in my absence. Any questions?" I asked, looking around the room.

When no one spoke, I stood up to leave.

"Ivy, thank you for getting on this so quick. I know you have a lot going on," Jeremy said, calmer than when I'd arrived.

"We're all family, and not long ago you all helped me when I needed it. I got your back no matter what. Stay safe," I replied, walking from the office with thoughts of cold-blooded murder on my mind. I tossed Big the keys and climbed in the passenger seat, already reaching for my phone because I had work to do.

"Dirty mother-*fucker!*" I growled through clenched teeth.

"Calm down, babe. You need to be clear-headed for this one."

"I know, but I saved that nigga's *life*, and this is how he repays me?"

"Don't worry, he's gonna get everything that's coming to him. We just gotta move smart so he doesn't see us coming," Big replied, starting the car and pointing us back in the direction of Fort Worth.

"Yeah, well the first thing we need to do is end this cat and mouse frame with the Sinaloa Cartel because trying to focus on multiple enemies will get us killed. And before you say it, I know I should've thought of that with the Gangsta Bit situation, and now our resources with the Gulf Cartel are spread thin."

"Now ain't the time for 'I told you so'," he replied wisely.

"Good decision. Now is the time for you to give me your honest opinion on how you think I handled shit back there."

"What do you mean? You know you made the best possible decision. Why are you second guessing it now?" he asked, giving me a bewildered look.

"I don't know, it's just, Jeremy's kid is in danger and if I make the wrong move, he dies. That's some heavy shit," I replied honestly.

"You know, before your dad was kidnapped, I used to wonder how you'd grown up with a father like him and remained so unaffected by everything around you. I mean, I know he kept you away from all the illegal shit, but you've never even seemed affected by the material things that come with this life. You were your own person, and I don't mean that to sound like a bad thing because it's something I've always loved about you. It's also something that made me feel like you'd never fit into this world because it would be like you putting on clothes that didn't fit. I was wrong about that. Everything that I've seen you do since your dad's kidnapping proves that I was wrong about that, and what I just saw back there was no different. You're your own person, but you're Soloman's daughter too, and you're *good* at this shit, bae. Don't *ever* doubt yourself," he said passionately.

His words gave me a feeling of warmth that I couldn't describe. He hadn't talked to me like I was just his girlfriend, but like I was his equal in a game that you were either built for or not. There was no in between. I may have had the weight of the world on my shoulders, but my man believed I could handle it, so I would.

"Thanks for the pep talk, bae," I said, smiling genuinely.

"No pep talk; just real talk. Now tell me what the next play is."

"I'm scheduling a meeting with Manuel because I'm gonna need his help for sure," I said, going through our emergency back channels on the internet to send him a message.

"I can put my homies to work too," Big offered.

"Would you have to go through Hoover Slim for that?"

"Nah, I'll make it happen myself. Just tell me what you need to do."

"Right now I need surveillance on this nigga Justice so I can find out what he's up to, see if I can figure out his end game. It's gonna be hard for your homies to do that because

I'm sure he's surrounded himself with his Piru connections," I replied.

"Money talks, sweetheart, plus I'm sure we have people who've infiltrated his organization. I can have him under a microscope without him knowing. Is that all you need?"

"Yeah, until I gather more information, because I have to make informed decisions only. Once Harley is home, we can do whatever we have to do to knock Justice's mu'fuckin' head off," I said enthusiastically.

"Do you know of any weaknesses we can exploit when it comes to him?"

"No...but Ebony might," I replied, immediately sending her a text message letting her know that I needed to talk to her as soon as we got back.

"You don't think she has anything to do with this, do you?" he asked, looking over at me.

"I don't know. It's obvious that he has to be moving off of some info she gave him when we were at war because he hasn't been around to know shit about my business. She could still be involved, or he could be acting on his own because his feelings are hurt that what I told him came true. All I know is she better *hope* she ain't in bed with that nigga."

Big didn't say anything else, but I could tell that we were thinking along the same lines. There was no way that either of us was gonna trust Ebony, and even though I had a backup plan for her ass should anything go wrong, I still didn't feel completely secure. With each mile we drove, it became clearer to me that I might have to put together a backup plan for my backup plan when it came to Ebony. The bitch just couldn't be trusted.

"Even if she's not in bed with him, do you think she'd actually help you exploit his weaknesses? I mean, this *is* the same nigga she called to the rescue when you had your high heel on her neck," Big said.

"I honestly don't know, bae. I don't feel like we hate each other enough to kill each other anymore, but I don't know what head space Ebony is in from one minute to the next. She's obviously all about Rock, and I *did* just save his life, so maybe she's feeling friendly towards me. Plus Justice was trying to come in between her and Rock."

"You can't forget that she blames you for Rock being in that situation, no matter *what* she may have told you," he reminded me.

The feeling of being able to trust no one around you was an exhausting one, and I closed my eyes for a moment while laying my head against the plush leather seat. My dad had warned me to watch everyone and everything around me, but somehow I'd let Justice slip off my radar. That was proving to be a costly mistake. I knew what he was capable of, which was the main reason that I didn't wanna provoke him, but it was obvious that he didn't know what *I* was capable of. This shit had the potential to end badly. My phone vibrating in my hand forced me to open my eyes, where I found a message from Manuel.

"Manuel is actually in Texas and says that we can meet," I informed Big.

"When and where?"

"I'm gonna suggest one of our restaurants. That way we have the privacy we need and a relaxed setting," I replied, already sending the message to him.

"Smart move. I guess you can just drop me off at home and handle your business."

"I told you before that I want you with me and that hasn't changed. Plus it don't make sense to go all the way back to Fort Worth when I told him we'd meet in Grand Prairie."

"Good thing you insisted that I dressed to impress at all times," he replied, smiling.

"*Now* you're getting it. Okay, so he just messaged and said that he can be there in an hour, which means I gotta call and have everything set up. Oh, and he's bringing his sister too, so - "

I had a sudden idea hit me like a lightning bolt, illuminating my problem with Justice and offering a possible path to a solution. "I know someone who knows Justice's weaknesses," I said, looking at Big.

"Who?"

"His sister. He has a half-sister," I replied, already searching for her on Facebook.

"Bae, what makes you think his own sister would betray him?"

"It's complicated, and I don't know that she will, but I know she's the only one who can get close to him right now without raising suspicion. It's worth a try, because we ain't got shit to lose."

## Chapter 14
## Ebony

"What makes you think that I'm trying to kill you?" Justice asked, sitting on the king-sized bed, trying not to smile

"Cut the bullshit, nigga, I recognized one of the mu'fuckas who shot at me and Rock outside the hospital earlier. He's dead, by the way. I can't believe you would actually send someone to kill me, Justice. What did I do to deserve that from you?"

"Like I said, what makes you think I was trying to kill you?" he asked again calmly.

"The shooter was one of your homies from Dallas! You can't deny that because he was with us the night we had that meet up with Ivy! You sent a hitta at me, and you ask what makes me think that you were trying to kill me? So am I supposed to believe that you were trying to *scare* me, and that way I'd come running to you for help?" I asked, getting angrier with every second he wore a dumb-ass innocent expression on his face.

"Ebony, you're not listening. What makes you think I was trying to kill *you*?"

"I *just fucking told you -* "

Suddenly the air and anger rushed from my body as I finally grasped what he'd been saying to me the whole time. I had been assuming that he'd been trying to kill me, but the smug look on his face while he watched my revelation taken ahold on me told me I'd been wrong. So wrong.

"Y-you were trying to kill Rockafella," I whispered, feeling my knees battle as my anger turned into a cold fury.

"It's not personal. It's business. You can understand that."

"You tried to kill the man I love, the man I just snatched back from death's icy grip, and you tell me that it's *not personal?*" I asked through gritted teeth.

"I didn't say that I didn't find the work distasteful. I simply said it was a business move I made. Your man has a nice bounty on his head, a million in cold cash, to be exact."

It was on the tip of my tongue to ask who put the money up, but I knew it wasn't Ivy, so that only left one other snake.

"There's no way you'd be working for Gangsta Bit. You two are from rival organizations," I said.

"This ain't the seventies, girl. The only color that matters in the world is *green,* and that nigga is offering up *a lot* of it for your dude. Why would I let someone else eat good when I can?"

"Because you supposed to fuck with me! Because you know what I just had to go through to get this nigga back alive! You're supposed to be my friend. Goddamn!"

"I *tried* being your mu'fuckin' friend and you shitted on me as soon as your nigga resurfaced!" he yelled, jumping up from the bed and getting in my face.

As long as I'd known Justice I'd never seen him put hands on any female, but I was quickly realizing I didn't know this man at all, so I took a step back.

"I didn't shit on you. I did what any real bitch would, and I made taking care of my man my top priority. I would've done the same for you and you *know* that."

"Nah, what I know is that I *did* do the same thing for you when you got shot. I was there for you through it *all*, Ebony. I went down to Texas as soon as you called without hesitation, and I didn't leave your side no matter *how* ugly shit got. You forgot about that though. You let that bitch Ivy get in your head and make you push me away," he said, shaking his head.

"Ivy got in my head? What the fuck are you talking about?" I asked, confused.

"Ivy told me that you didn't need me and you wouldn't want me around because Rock was back. She was right."

"No, that's not how I felt, and you should've fucking talked to me instead of getting on your bullshit," I said pointedly.

"I *tried* talking to you, but you was stuck up under that nigga's ass, so it is what it is."

"What does that mean, Justice? You're gonna kill Rock? You gonna kill me too?" I asked seriously.

For a minute the look in his eyes was blank and completely devoid of emotion, but then I saw a glimmer of the man I used to know.

"Even if I didn't kill Rockafella, that's not gonna take the price off his head."

"Maybe not, but maybe if you went to Gangsta Bit, you could somehow make that happen," I replied.

"And why would I do that?"

"Because you don't wanna see me hurt, and deep down, I know you still care about me," I replied truthfully.

"Caring about you cost me too much, and I can't see myself going back down that road. I'll make you a proposition though. You do something for me and I'll do something for you."

His statement was way too vague for my liking, and it had all the undertones of an indecent sexual proposal. What was I supposed to do though, let mu'fuckas keep gunning for me and my husband? We could always run far away, but what type of life could we have if we were always looking over our shoulders? I felt like I was in a no-win situation and at the mercy of niggas with no type of conscience. Sadly, I'd come too far to go back.

"What do you want me to do for you?" I asked hesitantly.

"It's two things actually, but one is easier than the other. Both benefit you though."

"Spit it out. I need to get back to Texas," I said with growing frustration.

"I want you to help me in my attack on Ivy and her business."

"Attack? What attack?" I asked, confused, yet intrigued.

"I've been making moves against Ivy and her business that she's running through the ports on the West coast. I started by hijacking a couple shipments, but I stepped it all the way up by going after her square-ass business associates. Now I'm in the driver's seat."

"Wowww, you a bold mu'fucka. Does Ivy know any of this?" I asked, somewhat impressed.

"She knows she's lost shipments, but she doesn't know it's me behind it. Her partner *definitely* ain't gonna say shit because he wants his son back alive."

"Oh, you just *all the way* on your bullshit, huh? What happened to playing it straight? Or did you say fuck parole too?"

"I know what I'm doing," he replied, retaking his seat on the bed.

"So what do you need from me? It seems like you got everything under control."

"I want to take *everything* from her - not just for me, but for you too. I'm not only talking about her money and power. I want her sanity. I want you to kill her father."

Hearing those words made my heart thunder in my chest, but I kept my outward appearance neutral. I didn't wanna entertain the madness this nigga was talking about, but my mind was already racing with scenarios on how to do it now that I had access to her house.

"What's your end game, Justice? How do you see this all playing out?"

"I see us finishing what she started when she pulled the trigger and killed your father. Deep down I *know* you ain't forgave her for that, so I don't know why you're letting her live the life you're supposed to have," he replied.

"I don't want her life. Rock and I have decided to play it straight, and I've got enough money to make sure we never want for anything."

"Money is no substitute for revenge," he stated simply.

I knew he was just trying to gas me up, and that meant I should've ignored him, but his words were the truth. No matter how wrong my dad had been, or what Ivy did to try and make it right, I couldn't forget what she'd taken from me. Nor could I forgive.

"Hypothetically, let's say I go along with your plan. What happens after Soloman dies?" I asked, sitting beside him on the bed.

"Then you rule beside me."

"Did you forget that I have a man?" I asked, having a bad feeling about where this conversation was going.

"Your man ain't got shit to do with me or the aftermath of this situation. I'm gonna be king, and you can choose to take your rightful position or you can sail off into the sunset with Rockafella. For me this is about business with a little bit of personal sprinkled in, but for you it's entirely more personal than business. So what do you want to do?"

We both knew the answer to what I *wanted* to do, so the real question was whether or not I was prepared to seize this opportunity. If I was being honest with myself, the decision had been made when he alluded to his ability to take the target off of Rock's head. I would do anything for my husband, and getting back at Ivy was simply a bonus.

"You said that there were two things you needed from me. What's the second?" I asked cautiously.

"I've missed you," he said softly, taking one of my hands in his. This time when my heart rate quickened, it was from anxiety and swiftly-building guilt.

"Justice…"

"I won't force you, EB. You know that ain't even how I get down. I know you love Rock and you're in love with him, but I know there's still some love for me in your heart. I know that because we were each other's first, and that's something you never get over. I'm not asking you to choose me over him. I'm simply asking that we start over by reliving a moment where we were great together," he said, moving closer to me.

When I looked up into his eyes, I did so with the intention of telling him that I didn't feel and ounce of anything romantic for him, but my words faltered. I could tell that he was looking at me through years of love and all the memories that came with that, and that made my heart beat with emotion that I dared not question. In my mind, this moment would only take place because I needed to save Rock, but I knew my heart would always call me a liar.

"I can't stay here with you all night. You know Ivy will be suspicious if I'm gone that long," I said softly.

"I'll have you back on your plane within the hour," he promised, taking my face in both of his hands and kissing me softly.

From the moment our lips touched, my brain started screaming in sheer panic, but it was for all the wrong reasons. It should've been because I was kissing a man who wasn't my husband on my wedding day, but instead the panic was because of my body's reaction to the kiss. My pussy was beating like an African drum, and it shouldn't have been! When he laid me down on the bed and moved in front of me

128

to pull my shorts off, I was hoping he'd just put his dick in and make this quick, but I should've known better. He started with soft kisses up my inner thighs, working his way slowly but steadily to his ultimate goal, and making it harder to breathe the whole way. When he arrived at his destination, he kissed my pussy lips in a way that made my mouth jealous, and I had to bite my tongue to keep from screaming out. His exploration of my private garden was tender, yet thorough enough to make me cum despite my chest efforts not to.

"Don't fight it, baby," he whispered right against my clit before he began flicking it wildly with his tongue.

My hands going to his head was an involuntary action, but suddenly I felt myself trying to pull him into my uterus and I couldn't stop. Ten minutes and two orgasms later, I didn't know what level of hell I'd be going to for this, but Justice had me beyond caring. While I was lying on the bed, still twitching uncontrollably, he picked me up and moved me to the center of the mattress. I watched in a fog as he undressed and slowly climbed on top of me, ashamed at how quickly I wrapped my legs around his waist and took him inside of me. It only took two strokes to know that the dick was better than I remembered, and I knew I had to fuck him quick so I wouldn't get hooked.

"D-don't fight it," I whispered, clenching my pussy walls every time he backed out of me.

I could see defeat in his eyes, but he kept trying to feed me those toe curling blows that had me trying to look up into my skull and see my brain. We battled for the longest fifteen minutes either of us had ever known before climaxing together in a haze of animalistic grunts and moans. As the sweat dried the guilt set in, and I knew I couldn't continue to lay here in bed with this man who wasn't my husband, so I hopped up and went to the shower. The blistering hot water couldn't cleanse me internally so I didn't take an extra-long shower for dramatic effect. I simply wasn't about to go home fortified for the awkward conversation I was destined to have to go through with Justice. I walked into the room to find him still ling in the bed, filling the room with weed smoke that still wasn't strong enough to cover up the smell of sex. I quickly got dressed before turning my attention to him.

"Now what?" I asked.

"Now you go back to Texas and act like nothing happened, and you wait on me to tell you when to move. Don't do anything to make Ivy suspicious."

"And what about Gangsta Bit?" I asked, needing clarity and conformation.

"I'll be meeting with him sometime tonight. Don't worry; I'll take care of it."

"Don't bullshit me, Justice, because I'm trusting you, and I'm not sure that I should," I confessed.

"You know you can trust me because if you didn't know that, we wouldn't have just slept together. You can tell yourself that you did it for your husband, but we both know that it was about you, and for more than one reason. Oh, and don't look so surprised that I referred to Rock as your husband, I noticed your ring right away."

"So this was about fucking another man's wife, huh?" I asked disgustedly.

"You know better than that. I didn't fuck you, EB. I made love to you, and the fact that you liked it is what has you feeling some type of way. Don't overanalyze this moment right now and get paranoid, thinking that I'm trying to ruin your marriage. I'm not. If you choose me it'll be *your choice.* For now, let's focus on us both getting what we want, and I'm sure everything else will fall into place, okay?"

I wanted to believe we could leave what had just happened between us right here in this hotel room, but I didn't see how that would be possible. It wouldn't be because of me though, and my actions were all I could control.

"Handle your business, Justice. I'm counting on you."

ARYANNA

## Chapter 15
## Ivy
## One month later

"Darlise Cole. Damn, bitch, it took your ass long enough to get out here," I said, hugging her tightly.

"Bitch, you *know* how stressful school is, and how much work had to be done. I can't just up and leave South Carolina when I feel like it."

"I hear you. I'm glad you made the trip though. You look good," I said, stepping back and looking her over from head to toe.

It had been more years than I could remember since I'd see Justice's little sister, but it was clear that the girl was now a woman. She only stood about 5'2" and weighed a slight 120 pounds, but she had an aura of sophistication about her that came with being comfortable in her own skin. Her chocolate brown complexion was smooth and without pimples, and her naturally curly hair framed her face in a way that screamed sex appeal. My only hope was that she was as mature as she looked because the game I played was for big girls only.

"I know I look good. Now come on in here," she replied, turning and walking back into her hotel room.

I wouldn't have minded her staying at my parents' house, but it was beyond a little crowded with Ebony and Rock still being there. Plus I didn't want Darlise and Ebony coming face to face because that would've inspired questions I didn't really want to answer. For a couple of reasons I hadn't told Ebony or Rock that Justice had been working overtime to dethrone me, mainly because I felt like if she knew something she'd tell on herself. I also didn't need her offering her services because she thought I couldn't handle everything that was coming my way. I was good, and getting better.

"So how are your grades?" I asked, taking a seat in one of the two overstuffed chairs sitting in the room.

"My grades are fine, *Mom*, how are yours?" she returned, sarcastically.

"I'm taking a break right now to run the family business."

"Yeah, I heard about that," she replied, sitting in the chair across from me.

"What else did you hear?"

"That you think you're better than everybody else, and you don't have to answer for the pain you caused, and blah, blah, blah," she said, shaking her head.

"Your brother sounds really bitter, but I don't get why," I said, genuinely confused.

"The common denominator seems to be Ebony. You're trying to come between him and Ebony, you're trying to get in her head and make her think that she doesn't need him. Oh, and you told her about you and Justice fucking around back in the day. Bitch, when were you gonna tell *me* that tea?"

"That shit is old news, and the only reason I put him on blast was because he came to Texas out of alleged loyalty to Ebony when her and I were at war," I replied dismissively.

"Yeah, I heard about that too. Did you really execute her dad and record it?"

I didn't give her a verbal response, but the look I leveled at her told the question was inappropriate, and the answer was, *hell yes*, I'd done it.

"No matter what happened between Ebony and I, I didn't have shit to do with her not fucking with your brother. She's *married*, for fuck's sake! I damn sure didn't make her do that. I wasn't even invited to the ceremony. Our relationship ain't *nothing* like it used to be, so there's no way I could sway her opinions, nor would I want to because I've got more important shit to worry about. Your brother is trippin'," I said, frustrated.

134

"That's not hard to believe. It wouldn't be the first time he's imagined a confrontation and acted on it."

Her statement was made from a truth that she knew only too well. To say her past with Justice was complicated was life's biggest understatement. They shared the same mother, but not the same father, and that was only the beginning of the complications because from the jump, Justice had been incapable of respecting a stepdaddy. He'd spent the better part of his life imagining that Darlise got treated better by her dad than he did, and that led to a resentment that morphed into hatred. One day Justice observed an argument between a man and wife, and that became the excuse he needed to take that man's life. Darlise had been too young to understand anything more than that her dad had gone to heaven, but her mother's deathbed confession after middle school exposed her to the truth about her beloved brother. It wasn't a truth that she could comprehend though because she'd loved her brother too much to see the evil in him, so she'd chosen to suppress the memory of her mother's last words. The only reason that I knew the truth was because a drunk persons words are a sober persons thoughts, and Darlise had brought that saying to life once upon a time. It stayed between her and me though.

"Does he wonder why you're suddenly communicating with him more?" I asked.

"No, he thinks I'm just making time for him because of all the time we lost while he was locked up."

"Does he trust you? Has he brought you into his business plans?"

"I mean, he tells me about all the money he's making, and he tries to spoil me. Does he trust me? Yeah. He's not offering me a seat at the table though. He's on my ass about finishing school," she replied.

"Of course he is. I'm telling you, that nigga is working my *last* nerve," I said, more than a little frustrated.

"I know. My position is the same though, Ivy. I'll help you anyway that I can, but I won't kill him and I won't help you kill him. Not for money or power," she said, determination clear in her voice.

"What about for revenge?" The look she leveled at me told me I was dangerously close to crossing a line in our friendship, but I'd honestly lost too much in the last month to play it safe any longer. When I'd approached her, I'd appealed to the fact that her brother had made a hostage out of a kid that wasn't a part of the street life, a kid only two years older than her. Darlise's compassion made her advocate for Harley, and she'd eventually get him returned to his family. That hadn't stopped Justice though, and that's what I needed to happen.

"I don't have any need for revenge, Ivy, that's not how I live my life."

"Not even for what happened to your father?" I asked pointedly.

"Don't go there. Don't try to exploit a situation you know nothing about for your own personal gain because it'll ruin our friendship," she warned with tears in her eyes.

I didn't know if I was seeing anger or pain manifest itself in front of me, but I couldn't back down for either at this point.

"I'm not trying to exploit anything, I'm simply speaking the truth. You of all people know how close Ebony and I were, but the pain I felt when I thought my father was dead made her just another bitch in my eyes. We were closer than blood, and still I didn't hesitate when it came to exacting my revenge. Are you really trying to tell me that you've forgiven Justice for killing your dad in cold blood?" I asked.

"What choice did I have, Ivy? Forgiveness isn't for anyone else, it's for you, and if I didn't forgive him, it would've destroyed me."

"Oh yeah? Did you *really* forgive him though, Darlise? I mean, you have been helping *me* for the last month, so what's the motivation behind that?" I asked thoughtfully.

"I can't *kill him* though! I just can't do that," she replied emphatically.

The sight of the tears she'd been holding back spilling onto her cheeks told me just how distressed she was over this whole situation. Her words rang with truth. She couldn't kill her brother, but she wanted to. In the quiet corners of her soul where she judged herself, she wanted to kill him.

"I'm not asking you to kill him. I can do that myself. He's just been impossible to get to," I said, frustrated.

"He's paranoid, you know that. Ever since he's gotten back on his bullshit, he's acting like he's back on the yard at Pelican Bay and everybody has a shank ready to stab him."

"I need to draw him out. Can you help me figure out how to do that?" I asked.

At first I took her silence as a sign that she was thinking of a way to help, but one look into her eyes told me that she had the solution all along.

"What aren't you saying, Darlise?"

"Before I answer that, I need you to agree not to hurt innocent people in your quest to get to Justice," she replied calmly.

"Define what you mean when you say innocent."

"Don't play games, Ivy, you know exactly what the fuck I mean," she said seriously.

"Fine, you have my word, now spill it."

Her eyes bore into mine, and I could tell that whatever she had to say was huge because she was apprehensive and more nervous than I'd ever seen her.

"He's got a female that he kicks it with, and I think it's serious," she said slowly.

"How serious?"

"She's a guard at the prison and I think they were fucking around when he was on the inside. She's got a seven-year-old little boy that looks just like Justice," she replied, reluctantly.

Hearing this told me that the relationship was more than serious. It had just become life and death.

"Where does she live, and how often does he see her?" I asked, scooting forward to the edge of the seat.

"Promise me you won't hurt the chick or my nephew before I tell you that."

"I promise no harm will come to them. It's him I'm after," I assured her.

"She lives in L.A., and he goes to visit at least once a week, sometimes even staying for the entire weekend."

"Do you have an exact address?" I asked, pulling my phone out of my pants pocket.

She pulled out her phone too and a few seconds later, I got a text with the address of one Ashlan Grant.

"Thank you, Darlise."

"Don't thank me. Just keep your promise not to hurt those who haven't done anything wrong except love the wrong man," she replied, wiping her eyes of leftover tears.

I know she was talking about herself as much as she was Justice's son and baby mama. I didn't feel like I'd hurt her in a literal sense, but I had caused her pain by bringing up a past that she would've rather left buried. Hopefully I could take that pain away not by erasing her brother from the Earth.

"How long can you stay out here?" I asked.

138

"My return flight is for Monday because I got class on Tuesday. Why?"

"Because I wanna take you out, spend some time with your crazy ass," I replied, smiling at her.

"Bitch, you just trying to get me drunk so you can laugh at me and pick my brain."

"No drinking, I promise. We'll simply go have some food and some girl time at one of my restaurants."

"Listen at you, Miss businesswoman. That sounds like a plan, but not tonight though because I'm exhausted," she replied, stifling a yawn.

I took that as my cue to leave and I stood up. She followed my lead and walked me to the door, where we embraced again.

"It's good to see you, and not just because you've been helping me out either. I've missed you, and I'm sorry I waited so long to reach out," I said genuinely.

"It's okay. I could've called you or hit you up on Facebook too. No matter what happens, we'll keep in touch from now on, agreed?"

"Agreed," I replied, hugging her one last time before leaving her room.

The moment I stepped onto the elevator and the door closed, my mind switched over to work. I didn't have time to waste when it came to putting a plan together for concerning Justice because he was *definitely* becoming a pain in my ass. I sent Big a text first letting him know that I'd be home soon. My next move would be to text Manuel when I got to my car, but when I came out of the elevator into the parking garage, I was met by a beefy Mexican in a black suit.

"Manuel wants to see you," the man stated.

It was clear that his words weren't spoken with an option for refusal, and looking past him I could see a black Hummer idling.

"Okay, where is he?" I asked.

I was led to the back of the Hummer, where the door was opened, and I climbed in next to the lone figure who was puffing on a cigar. The way this whole thing was going down was causing my stomach to knot up like I had to shit, but I played it cool because men like Manuel fed on fear.

"This is a surprise," I said casually.

"It was intended to be. How are you?"

"I'm good, how are you?" I asked, hoping to project the vibe of this being a normal conversation. Deep down I knew it was anything but normal Shit, just the fact that he knew where I was at 11 o'clock at night was proof enough. Manuel may have been a slight built, soft spoken man with a head full of shimmering white hair, but he wasn't one you played for stupid or underestimated.

"I'm good too. Actually better than good because I come to bring you two types of news. One you will find good, and the other I think you will find interesting. The good news is that Esteban has retired - permanently," he said.

"You know this for certain?"

"Why would you insult me with such a question?" he replied, blowing a thick stream of smoke in my direction.

"I didn't mean to insult you. It's just hard to believe it's over after all the failed attempts to get to him."

"It wasn't easy by any means, and it came with collateral damage, but in the end we emerged victorious and that's what's important," he insisted.

"I agree. What's your other news?" I asked, feeling less apprehensive about his surprise visit.

"Well, now that Esteban in no longer a problem, it's time for you to hold up your end of the bargain with regards to your distribution of our merchandise."

"Of course, there's absolutely no problem with that," I replied reassuringly.

"Ah, but there is a problem. How can I trust you with billions of dollars of merchandise when you are under attack by someone intent to take over your empire?"

The only thing that hid my surprise was the fact that we were sitting in a dark truck, but I knew the expression on my face was one that screamed "what the fuck" in any language. I knew I had to choose my words wisely or risk fucking up more than a business relationship.

"I'm handling that situation," I said calmly.

"Why did I not know there *was* a situation," he returned quickly.

"I'd already come to you about the situation with Gangsta Bit, plus you were still waging a war against the Sinaloa Cartel. I didn't want to spread you and your people too thin," I rationalized.

"Did I not take care of Gangsta Bit two weeks ago?"

Hearing the question brought back the images of cops finding pieces of Gangsta Bit in the four corners of states of North America, and them having no idea who killed him.

"Yes you did, and I could've told you then, but I had it under control. As a matter of fact, I just got the information I needed to draw my enemy out and put an end to the bullshit," I replied.

"That's good. And you won't mind sharing your plan with me, right?"

I was smart enough to know that what he said wasn't a question or a request. It was a demand. After taking a deep breath, I ran down to him what Darlise had passed along to me, making it clear that I intended to handle the situation immediately.

"If this doesn't work, do you have a backup plan?" he asked.

"It'll work," I stated, confidently.

"Ms. Black, we have done good business and it is my hope that we can continue to do so. In order for that to happen, there must be no secrets between us as it pertains to business because ultimately what affects your business affects mine. Understand?"

"I understand completely, and - "

"Good. To demonstrate your understanding, I want you to give me the information you have and I'll take care of the rest. In the meantime, I want you to focus on our collaborative business interests, okay?"

"No problem," I replied.

"Good. I'm glad we understand each other."

## Chapter 16
### Ebony

"Baby, if you don't get up, I'm leaving you here," I warned, climbing out of the bed and walking naked into the bathroom. After turning the shower on to let the water get hot like I liked it, I quickly brushed my teeth, hoping to save time by multitasking. My doctor's appointment wasn't for another hour, but getting out of this fortress called a house was a lengthy ordeal sometimes. Even with Gangsta Bit being dead, Ivy still insisted that Rock and I stick close to the house or move with a lot of security, because the Sinaloa Cartel was gunning for everybody. I hadn't told her or Rock that Justice had been behind the hospital shooting, nor had I told the cops when they finally came calling. After viewing the hospital camera footage, the cops immediately concluded that I'd been defending myself, but they were more interested in why there had been multiple attempts on my life. I couldn't answer that question any more than I could the one about the identity of the shooters. As we'd hoped, the cops closed their investigation within a couple weeks, but none of us had any doubts about whether or not we were still under police observation. Rock and I were preparing to leave, depending on what my doctor had to say during my follow-up appointment today.

"You ain't even in the shower yet," Rock said, slapping my ass when he walked past me and through the open shower door. I finished what I was doing and followed his lead, pulling the door closed behind me.

"I know how long it takes your slow ass to get moving, and we ain't got time to waste," I said, taking the soap from his hands.

"We've got a little time," he replied, backing me into the shower door before lifting me into the air.

"Babe, I'm having a full exam in an hour. We can't have sex," I told him reluctantly. The passion in his eyes made it clear just how bad he wanted to be inside me, but he put me back on my feet anyway and took the soap back.

"Did you talk to Ivy last night?" he asked, soaping up my body slowly and thoroughly.

"No, she wasn't home when I went downstairs. I'm gonna talk to her today though."

"Good, because it's time for us to do our own thing. I *never* thought that we would be here this long, and I'm tired of being cooped up in the house like some child."

"I know, babe, me too, but you know it was necessary," I replied, fighting the rising heat in my body as he continued touching me innocently.

"Yeah, well, Gangsta Bit is gone, and I'm back to being one hundred percent so we're good to be on our own."

I couldn't argue with how quickly he'd healed - not just physically, but mentally as well. Rock was definitely back to his old self, which meant that he wasn't nobody's bitch and he damn sure wasn't about to live like one. The only problem I had with that was the fact that I *needed* to be in this house a little longer to help with the most important part of Justice's plan. Our alliance was still a closely kept secret, and surprisingly enough Ivy seemed none the wiser about what was going on right under her nose. I'd stressed for days that I'd made the wrong decision, not just about agreeing to be a part of Justice's scheme, but about sleeping with him too. In one night I'd put my future in the hands of a man that couldn't be trusted, but so far he hadn't betrayed the trust. Just a little longer and it would all be over.

"I was thinking that we'd go to Bora Bora for a month and relax for a while," I said, taking the soap back and bathing him.

"That's what you were thinking, huh? To be honest, babe, I don't give a fuck where we go just as long as we're together *and* alone," he replied, pulling me against him and kissing me softly.

The heat of his mouth melted away the little bit of will power I had left, and ten minutes later we both stepped out of the shower with satisfied grins.

"I still miss the bathtub in Ivy's bedroom," I confessed, walking back into the guest bedroom we'd been sharing for the last three weeks.

"Well, baby, you were the one who said it was weird to be fucking in her bed."

"It *was*, but that tub experience was a-maz-ing!"

"Damn, you make it sound like you didn't like the pounding I just gave you. I mean, I know I pulled out and came on your ass cheeks, but that was so your doctor didn't think you were trifling for showing up to an OB/GYN appointment leaking cum," he replied, laughing hard.

"Whatever, Negro, just hurry up and get dressed," I said, laughing with him while picking through my clothes in the closet.

After we'd all determined that our stay here would be for an indefinite amount of time, Rock and I had done a lot of on-line shopping. It killed two birds with one stone because we had our own clothes to wear now, plus we didn't have to worry about shopping before we took off. After putting on a baby blue thigh high summer dress with matching suede high heels, I left Rock to get dressed while I was in search of Ivy. As expected, I found her in her dad's office.

"Do you ever sleep?" I asked, strolling into the room.

"When I can. What's got you up and dressed before noon?"

"I've got a doctor's appointment, just a checkup and exam because of all the surgery I had. I came to tell you about it last night, but you weren't home," I replied, watching her closely.

"Yeah, I had an unexpected meeting. What time is your appointment?'

"10 a.m. Can you spare the personnel to accompany Rock and me?"

"That ain't necessary. You can just take my car and go," she replied casually.

Her statement made me pause because it could only mean one of two things. Either all threats had been neutralized, or she was simply willing to throw us to the wolves.

"Why the change all of a sudden?" I asked, sitting in the chair across the desk from her.

"Things have changed. There's no more danger to you or your husband, so you can move around just like normal."

"Really? So we can move out then?" I asked.

"Of course you can. You're not a prisoner, Ebony."

Even though she'd stated why things had changed, I really wanted more details, but I knew I had to be careful so I wouldn't draw suspicion.

"It's hard to believe the war is actually over. It seems like a lifetime ago when all we had to worry about was final exams," I said.

"I know. At least now you can finish up with school if you want."

"You're not gonna consider doing the same thing? I mean, if there are really no threats against us, then things can return to some semi balance of normal for you too," I reasoned.

"No, it can't. This is the life I've chosen now, and I'm okay with that because I'm prepared to handle what comes with it," she replied confidently.

Something about the self-assured look on her face annoyed me in a major way. I hadn't made a big deal about her hostile takeover of the illegal business that *both* of our fathers had helped build because Rock and I had decided to live a different kind of life. However, hearing her talk like it was a foregone conclusion that she would rule over the empire alone was making my ass itch in frustration.

"I'm glad things have calmed down now because that means Rock and I can rebuild in Houston once we get back from our honeymoon. I know the president is still bitching about the opioid epidemic, but we can get things up and running if we do it the right way," I said casually.

"What are you talking about Ebony?"

"I'm talking about picking up the slack in my father's old areas. Or are we not in this together anymore?"

My question caused her to look at me through narrowed eyes, and that made me smile on the inside. I was being petty, but the bitch shouldn't just be making assumptions that I was gonna let her dismiss me and all the work my father had put in.

"Are you saying that you wanna work for me?" she asked.

"*Work* for you? What the fuck are talking about? We'd be partners," I replied, laughing lightly without humor.

"Partners? EB, you're not being serious right now. Do you actually believe my suppliers would continue dealing with me if they knew that you were involved in the business, after *everything* you've done?"

"Everything *I've* done. You seem to forget that *you've* done more fucking damage than - "

"EB, calm down, and just *think* for a second! We're not talking about a legal business with legal business partners. We're talking about mu'fuckas who would make their own *mothers* disappear if they couldn't trust them, and you want me to go to them explaining that we're all good? That you can be trusted not to disrupt their business again? How do you see that conversation going?" she asked calmly.

I wanted to scream at her that I didn't give a fuck how the conversation went or what she had to explain because the business was built on *our* fathers' backs. The rational part of me stopped me from screaming though because I understood the validity of what she said. As long as the Gulf Cartel had her as their first option, they wouldn't be able to see me or what I could bring to the table. I would simply have to turn on some light so I wouldn't be cast in her shadow.

"I get what you're saying, I just thought that we could work together like our fathers did. In truth, it's not the business I was hoping to rebuild, it was us. I just felt like this would be another way to bring us closer, you know?" I said, projecting a calm that I didn't entirely feel.

"I feel that, sis. I miss how we used to be every single day and I want that back. So I'm not saying no; I'm saying not right now because I need to restore calm and confidence in the business. Once that's done we can talk about this again, okay?"

Her placating tone was like nails on a chalkboard, but I managed not to wince or show my true feelings about what she had to say.

"Okay. I need to get going so I'm not late for my appointment. Which car do you want me to take?"

"Take the Aston Martian. It's my wedding present to you and Rock," she replied, smiling.

"What?" I asked, pausing in my motion to stand up.

"You heard me. And I've already had the title switched to your name, so you can't refuse my gift."

I opened my mouth to say something, but only air came out because I was actually speechless. The moment I had Ivy figured out for the selfish, entitled bitch that she was, she did something to make me question myself, and I didn't like that.

"Uh, thank you," I replied hesitantly, still caught off guard.

"It's nothing. You're welcome to stay here as long as you need. Just let me know when you make other plans."

"I will," I said, getting up and walking out of the room before my confused emotions got the better of me.

"There you are. Are you ready to go?" Rock asked, running into me in the hall.

"Yeah," I replied distractedly, leading the way through the house to the garage.

"Are we not waiting on the ever-present security entourage?" he asked once we were in the garage.

"No. Get in."

Thankfully, he did what I told without asking any questions, but I could tell by the look he was giving me that he badly wanted to. After retrieving the car keys, I got behind the wheel and we were on the move.

"You can start talking at any time now," he said once we'd passed through the front gates.

"I'm not even sure where to start."

"You can start with how we just travelled outside the prison walls without our guards," he replied, looking behind us to verify we were really on our own.

"Ivy said the threats have been taken care of, we have nothing to worry about, and we're free to move out when we want to."

"Is that really all the details she gave you?"

"Yeah. She doesn't wanna talk about the business with me. She doesn't want me involved in the business at *all*," I replied bitterly.

"I thought we were moving past that, babe."

"We are, but *she* doesn't know that, which means she's making the decision to keep everything for herself. Selfish bitch," I growled.

"So what are you saying, you wanna go at her again?"

His question caused me to look over at him to gauge how he felt about that idea, and I could tell he would back whatever my play was."

"I don't know what I'm saying right now other than I need a vacation. I'm tempted to walk out of this doctor's office, point the car north, and put my foot on the gas," I said seriously.

"I'm with the vacation idea, but stealing Ivy's car is a bad idea."

"Oh, I didn't tell you? Ivy gave us this car as a wedding present," I replied.

The look of surprised confusion on Rock's face was probably the same one I'd had on my face when Ivy offered the gift, and it was almost comical.

"Do you think it's her way of buying you off?" he asked.

"I haven't thought of that, but now that you mention it, I don't put it past her sneaky ass."

"Well, when you decide what you wanna do you, I'm behind you one hundred percent, no matter what. It's *always* us against the world, babe," he said, taking my free hand in his.

I squeezed his hand reassuringly, and we rode the rest of the way to the doctor's office joined like that. We arrived five minutes before my appointment and were shown straight into the octopus exam room as soon as we walked through the door.

"Ms. Dahl, how are you feeling today?" Dr. Crith asked, coming through the door five minutes later.

"I'm good, doc, no lingering pain or anything."

"That's good to hear. I was hoping you would make a full recovery after your traumatic incident. So let's examine you to make sure that's the case. I need you to change into one of those hospital gowns over there and then hop up onto the table," he instructed.

It felt weird to have Rock in the room watching what was about to take place, but I knew shit would get ugly if I suggested he leave. I quickly got undressed, put the paper thin gown on, and climbed on the exam table while putting my feet in the stirrups.

"Okay, let's see what we got," Dr. Crith said, putting gloves on and lifting my gown.

I was surprised to feel Rock take my hand and divert my attention to him, but I was thankful. I was familiar with having a Pap smear done, but it was a cold and clinical procedure, and Rock being here changed that. I loved having a husband that I could go through anything with.

"Well, everything seems fine, but there's one other thing that I wanna do," Dr. Crith said after a relatively brief examination.

"Uh, okay," I replied, looking at Rock, trying to hide the concern that was creeping in.

"It's okay, Ms. Dahl, it's standard to do an ultrasound after having a operation on your stomach that was the result of a gunshot. I want to make sure nothing was missed and that there are no signs of an infection. It'll only take a minute."

Once he had the machine turned on and the cold-ass jelly on my stomach he moved the wand back and forth slowly. I

ARYANNA

couldn't look at the doctor or the ultrasound screen because both would remind me of the child I'd lost, and I could already feel that pain pressing in on me.

"It's okay, sweetheart, I'm right here," Rock whispered, wiping tears from my eyes that I didn't realize were leaking from my eyes.

"No need to worry at all, Ms. Dahl, everything is perfectly okay, and you'll be able to carry to full term," Dr. Crith said.

"Wh-what are you talking about? Carry what?" I asked, confused.

"The baby. You're definitely pregnant."

# Chapter 17
## Ivy

"What you watching on TV, Dad?" I asked, creeping into his room. I could tell by the look on his face that I'd caught him doing something he wasn't proud of.

"It's nothing, just daytime television," he replied evasively.

I happened to look up at the screen just as the words *General Hospital* rolled across in bold letters.

"Ooooh, you laid up in here watching a soap opera!" I teased, laughing and sitting by his bed.

"Shut up and stop judging me because you don't know what be going on. It's some gangsta shit happening."

"Whatever you say. Now I know for sure that I'ma have to start getting you out of the house because you're losing yourself in a world of make believe," I replied, muting the volume on the TV so we could talk.

"Get me out of the house, huh? Is it safe for us to try that?"

"I believe so. The situation with the Sinaloa Cartel has been taken care of, and the partnership with the Gulf Cartel is looking beautiful for the future."

"Okay, so what aren't you telling me?" he asked.

"There's another little situation, but Manuel came to see me personally last night to let me know that his people would take care of it. He wants my focus on the business and not the bullshit."

"That's because he's smart. You were never supposed to be in the streets sweetheart. You were supposed to get the education that allows you to rule over them from afar. I know things didn't go exactly as planned, but now it's about moving forwards and not backwards. I wish you didn't have to do any illegal business, but you've gotta keep your word to those who've showed you loyalty when you needed it most. For dudes like Manuel, it's not only about the money, it's about loyalty. Loyalty is everything," he said sincerely.

"No, it's guilt. You feel like you took everything from her, but you didn't. At the end of the day, it was you that saved her life, so that should counter the guilt you feel. I'm curious to know what brought up that question now though?"

"We just had a conversation not too long ago, and she wants us to work together like you and Jacob used to. She thinks that'll help to rebuild our relationship, and she's offered to pick up the slack in Houston," I replied.

"And you said?"

"I told her it wasn't realistic because the people I'm in business with only deal with people they trust, and she's done *way* too much for them to trust her," I replied, honestly.

My father's sigh of relief was long and audible.

"You had me worried for a second. I thought you were gonna wax poetic on some sentimental shit," he said seriously.

"No. I mean, I do miss my friend and my sister, but it would be naïve of me to believe I could ever have either of those things back. I gonna keep my eyes focused firmly on the future."

"And what does the future look like? What do you envision five years from now?" he asked curiously.

"Well…businesswise I expect that our net worth will be well into the billions, as long as everybody plays their positions and no one gets greedy. When it comes to my personal life, I think Big and I will be married by then."

"You seemed surer of the business plans than your personal ones. Is everything okay between you and Big?" he asked, concerned.

"We're good. I mean, everything that has happened has brought us closer than ever before. And I love him beyond words."

"But?" he prompted.

The next words I was about to speak made me pause. My dad and I didn't have secrets, but some topics of conversation were more personal than others.

"I stopped taking my birth control pill months ago, and I'm still not pregnant," I blurted, averting my gaze so I didn't have to see the judgement and embarrassment in my dad's eyes.

"You're, uh, you're trying to get pregnant?"

"I am, but Big doesn't know that I stopped taking my pills," I replied slowly.

"Wait, are you trying to trick him? Are you worried he'll leave or - "

"No, Dad, it's not like that. It's just…life is so precious, so *fleeting.* You're here, but nothing about the next moment is promised to *any* of us. My life is different now, and I no longer have the safety you provided or the option to be on the sideline, so if I leave this world tomorrow, I don't want it to be without experiencing my greatest joy. I wanna be a mom, but the fact that I'm not pregnant already is worrying me," I confessed sadly.

"Baby, you can't be worried that it hasn't happened yet. First of all, you know stress ain't good when it comes to trying to get pregnant, and you've *definitely* been under your fair share of stress. Secondly, the miracle of childbirth is not in your hands, despite what you could do to get pregnant. It's God's will and it'll happen in *his* time, not yours. Just be patient, okay?"

"I'll do my best, but you know that's not one of my strong suits. Do you think I should talk to Big about this?" I asked.

"Normally I'd say yes because you two work through everything together. But I don't think so this time because it'll just add stress and pressure to your relationship. I know you don't want that."

My dad was right about that because borrowing trouble was a recipe for disaster in a relationship. There was no need to have the conversation with Big about us not being pregnant because it would inevitably lead to a doctor's office and a battery of tests. I'd rather exercise extreme patience than put my relationship through that.

"Do you know how glad I am that I can talk to yo about anything, even really personal things?" I asked, smiling at my dad.

"I'm glad too, sweetheart. Just a piece of advice though: you better pray for sons because having daughters will cause you *a lot* more worry."

"Very funny, Dad! Are you gonna be okay for a while? I think I'm gonna take my man to lunch," I said, standing up.

"I'll be fine. Just make sure you turn that volume back up on my TV show."

I did like I was told, laughing the whole time. I was still laughing when I found Big in the backyard, laughing by the pool.

"Look at you, looking like a kept man."

"I guess that makes you my sugar mamma then, doesn't it?" he replied, smiling widely.

"Yeah right, nigga, you *know* I don't do no trickin', not even on you!"

"Don't worry, I'll earn my keep," he promised, pulling me onto his lap in the lounge chair.

"Oh really? When would you like to start?"

"I'd start now if we didn't have so many guests in this house," he replied, kissing my neck softly.

I always loved the feeling of being in his arms, but it was more intense when he had no shirt on and I could feel those muscles rippling against me.

"Well lucky for you, Ebony and Rock just left, and I've downsized our security, so if you want to…" I said, letting my sentence hang in the air while slipping my hand into his swimming trunks and grabbing something familiar.

"You need to come up out of those pants then," he said, quickly unbuttoning my slacks. After looking around to make sure no eyes were pointed in our direction I stood up and wiggled out of my pants, leaving me in my white blouse and purple boy shorts. I wasted no time straddling Big, and he wasted even less time pulling my panties aside and guiding his throbbing dick deep inside me.

"Mmm, we meet again," I whispered, kissing him passionately while moving in slow circles.

"Yes we do, and I missed you, baby."

We'd just found our rhythm when my phone started going off. I ignored it and let it ring through to voicemail, but then it started ringing again insistently and it was throwing me off.

"Y-you can answer it, b-but I'm n-not stopping," Big warned, gripping my ass cheeks tightly and pumping harder.

I let it keep ringing, figuring that whoever was calling would take the hint after twenty unanswered rings. I was wrong.

"Mmm, fuck!" I yelled, leaning over and grabbing my phone out of my pants pocket. True to his word, Big didn't miss a stroke or stop putting a much needed punishment on my pussy walls.

"H-hel-lo," I answered breathlessly.

"We need to meet. Come to my compound in Waco," Manuel demanded, hanging up before I could reply.

"Shit," I mumbled.

"Who was that?"

"Manuel," I replied shortly, tossing my phone on top of my pants so I could use both hands to hold onto Big. Suddenly he pulled his legs up in a way that almost threw me head first over the lounge chair, but he held on to me tight and kept serving up full strokes of good dick.

"My-my G-G-G spot!" I cried out as my eyes rolled into the back of my skull in pure bliss. It was like riding a roller coaster where every drop made you wanna cum instead of piss on yourself I excitement, and I enjoyed the ride all the way down.

This time when my phone started ringing I was physically incapable of answering it because the wave of my first orgasm had me pinned to the ocean floor. Moments later I felt Big cum inside me, but his dick stayed hard enough for me to ride my aftershocks into another explosion that left me breathless. Thankfully by the time I collapsed on his chest my phone had stopped ringing because all I wanted was to lay right where I was.

"I n-needed that," I confessed in a hoarse whisper.

"We both did. I actually think we need more."

"Just give me a m-m-minute," I pleaded, fully aware that he was still very much inside me.

"I ain't going nowhere, bae, and neither are you," he replied, laughing softly while wrapping his arms around me. Much to our mutual annoyance my phone started ringing again, and even though I didn't want to, I knew I had to answer.

"Yeah?

"Call me from a secure line *now*," Manuel ordered, again handing up before I could say anything back.

"Goddamn it!" I exclaimed, reluctantly climbing off of Big and quickly putting my pants on.

"What's wrong, babe?"

"I don't know, but that's the second time he's called, which means somethings up. I'll be right back," I said, hurrying into the house and going straight for the secure phone that I kept in the safe. After closing the door, I hurriedly dialed Manuel's number and waited.

"What's going on?" I asked once he answered.

"I'm going back to Mexico for a little while, just until shit calms down. I expect you to keep things moving in the right direction, and under *no* circumstances are you to engage in any street conflict."

"Okay. Why do you think that I *would* be involved in any street conflicts?" I asked warily.

"I'm not assuming that you would be. I'm telling you that I want your focus on business. If anything should come up, my people will continue to handle it, and I will monitor everything from Mexico. My most trusted lieutenant will be in contact with you and at your disposal. And just so we're clear, more money, more business, and more responsibility on your part means less room for error and no room for mistakes. Understood?"

"I got it, Manuel, don't worry. When should I expect to hear from you lieutenant? I asked, getting a bad feeling.

"Soon, and he'll be reporting to me daily. I will contact you as needed," he replied, disconnecting our call abruptly.

I had no idea what that was all about, but I knew it was *definitely* too weird to be nothing. I put the phone back in the safe and was about to go back outside to Big when my phone started ringing again.

"Now what?" I wondered aloud, before answering.

"Hello?"

"Y-you promised! You p-promised, bitch!" a shrill voice yelled at me.

"What?" I asked, confused, looking at my phone and the number the call was coming from. I didn't recognize it.

"You fucking *promised*, Ivy! You looked me right in the eyes and *promised*!" the voice yelled emotionally.

It was hard trying to make sense out of the hysterical crying following the angry words, but I was at least able to recognize the voice.

"Darlise, is that you?" I asked, feeling touches of panic.

"Stop playing dumb, bitch, you know it's me! You know what you did, and you'll burn in hell for it, I *promise*!" she replied, hanging up on me.

The whole exchange left me staring at the phone in my hand utterly lost, with a rising feeling of dread making my stomach turn. I had no idea what that call was about, but something told me I'd soon find out and it wouldn't be good. I opened the door to my dad's office to find his primary nurse standing on the other side with her fist raised, preparing to knock.

"What is it, Alissa?" I asked, immediately concerned.

"Your father instructed me to come and get you right away."

Pushing past her, I made a mad dash for his room, feeling my heartbeat in my throat in anticipation of what I might find.

"Dad, Dad are you okay?" I asked as soon as I came in the room.

"I'm fine. Close the door and come here," he replied calmly. A little *too* calmly.

"I didn't hesitate with my movements and I was seated in the chair by his side within seconds.

"What is it, Dad?"

"Earlier you told me that you had another *little* problem, but Manuel was gonna take care of it. Look at the TV and please tell me that that's not our problem."

I turned to look at the screen and what I saw put the last two calls I'd had into clear perspective, and it was all bad.

"Oh fuck. What have they done?"

# ARYANNA

## Chapter 18
## Ebony

"I'm sorry, did you just say I was pregnant? As in right now there is a baby growing inside me?" I asked, dumbfounded.

"Indeed, there is. You're about six or seven weeks along by my calculations, but your response tells me that you had no idea," Dr. Crith replied, smiling.

"No, doc, we didn't," Rock said slowly, clearly as shocked as I was.

"Well congratulations to you both, and I pray that this time there are no unfortunate circumstances that prevent you from fully realizing this miracle. I'll print you out a picture of the ultrasound I just did, and you can pick it up from my receptionist on your way out, along with your next appointment card."

"Th-thank you, doctor," I replied, still dazed and trying to process the information I'd been given. I was *pregnant*, actually *pregnant*! With all my heart and soul I'd wanted a do over, but it wasn't something I'd even had the courage to bring up to Rock since getting him back. Deep down I knew that he probably wanted what I did, but to talk about it would've meant facing the fact that it might not have happened, and that was too harsh of a reality. The one moment of vulnerability I'd had he did promise that we'd have a baby, and he'd been true to his word.

"Baby, we're pregnant," I said, looking at him with tears blurring my vision.

"Yes we are," he replied, smiling proudly and leaning in to kiss me.

I know he meant the joining of our mouths to be innocent, but I attacked his lips in hunger and pulled him towards me.

"I need you," I murmured, already pulling at the zipper to his jeans.

"Here? Right now?"

"Yes, just lock the door," I instructed, pushing him so he'd move faster.

I quickly pulled my legs out of the stirrups, but made sure to keep them spread wide open for him while pulling my gown up higher. I heard the lock click and when he turned around his dick was already out, making it clear to see that his third eye was matching the hunger I saw blazing in the other two. Any other time my pussy would've been gushing just because of how he was looking at me, and moving towards me like a cop with a battering ram, but right now it wasn't. I'd seen that same look of desire in another man, and that flash of insight had me suddenly doing math in my head.

"Baby, baby, wait!"

I couldn't get my words out quick enough to stop the first blow he delivered, and the dick felt so good that I lost all focus for a minute.

"Rock, w-we gotta stop," I said, pushing weakly on his chest.

"Stop? Why, am I hurting you?" he asked, immediately panicked.

"No, but, um, didn't the doctor say I was only a month along? I don't want to do anything that could jeopardize the baby," I replied lamely.

"Oh. Well, I can always go slower," he offered, pushing inside me inch by inch to demonstrate what he had in mind.

"Th-that's good, baby, but it doesn't work for a quickie in the doctor's office, so we need to finish this somewhere else," I replied, reluctantly pushing him back again. I was equally relieved and thankful when he simply smiled in agreement, pulled his dick out of me, and put it away.

"Can you go grab the ultrasound picture and appointment card while I get dressed?" I asked.

"Of course. I'll meet you out there."

Once he was gone I had to force the hysteria I was feeling *way* down because I was on the verge of losing my goddamn mind! Being four weeks pregnant meant the baby could be Rock's *or* Justice's, and that was *not* a reality that I knew how to deal with! Just entertaining the thought had me wanting to cry and vomit at the same time, but I knew neither thing would help with my current situation. How could I have been so *stupid*? Not only had I made myself a statistic, but I'd put myself in an impossible situation that could cost people their lives. I had no doubt that Rock would kill Justice before he played the role of stepdaddy to his child, and Justice would try to kill Rock equally as quick. And since having an abortion was absolutely out of the question the only outcome that was acceptable was Rock being the biological father. It was too early to get a DNA test, but that was okay because I was in *no* hurry to deal with the ugliness of truth. For now the best thing I could do was take care of myself and the baby inside me because there was no way I could lose another child. I wasn't strong enough to handle that. After a few deep breaths to settle my nerves I was finally able to climb down off the table and put my clothes back on. Once that was done, I made my way back to the reception area, where I found Rock waiting for me, holding a bottle of orange juice.

"Okay, I wasn't back there long enough for you to run to the store, so where did you get that from?" I asked.

"I may have made the receptionist an offer she couldn't refuse, but don't worry, I didn't mix any champagne with it yet."

"Very funny. You think our baby wants a mimosa?"

"Only if that's orange juice and apple cider," he replied, smiling.

"Ugh, that don't even sound good. What *would* sound good is some breakfast, so would you mind taking us somewhere to eat please?"

"You know I got you," he said, taking my hand and leading us out of the doctor's office.

Not surprisingly, he led me straight to the passenger side of the car, took the keys, and put me in before getting in the driver's seat. I knew this was only the beginning of him waiting on me hand and foot, and it already felt like the guilt would choke me to death. I had to fight it and appear normal because the *last* thing I wanted to do was make Rock suspicious, or make him feel like I was unappreciative. I'd spend every day for the rest of our lives making up for my mistake and proving to my husband that he was the one true love of my life.

"So where are we going?" I asked once he had us on the road.

"Well, if I know you like I think I do, then I figure some good Waffle House is in order, but after that you'll just have to trust me."

"Oh Lord, what do you have up your sleeve now, boy?" I asked suspiciously.

"Don't worry about all that. You're in good hands, so relax your mind."

That was definitely a task that was easier said than done, but I put a smile on my face and convinced myself to simply go with the flow. Twenty minutes later we arrived at the Waffle House and I was allowed to get elbow deep in fried chicken drizzled in maple syrup, accompanied by a snack of fluffy apple cinnamon waffles. Being pregnant gave me the perfect excuse to stuff my face like a big bitch at a buffet, and I took advantage of it unapologetically.

"Damn, did the doctor say we were having twins when I wasn't listening?" Rock asked, smiling at me over his own plate of chicken and waffles.

"Fuck you, don't judge me. And you better love me when I can't see my feet too, nigga, or I'ma put a fat foot up your ass," I promised, laughing and going back to my food.

"I'ma love you *for life*, babe, you already know that, and yes that includes when you can't see your feet. I won't just give you foot rubs. I'll still be sucking them toes too."

I almost choked on my chicken at this declaration, but I didn't put it down. I was halfway through my second chicken breast when my phone started going off, forcing me to finally come up for air, but I wasn't happy about it. It took so long to wipe my hands that I thought the phone would stop ringing, but as soon as it did it started right back.

"Damn, somebody is serious about talking to you. I hope it ain't Ivy," Rock said in between bites of waffles. Looking at the area code that the call was coming from I knew it wasn't Ivy, but talking to her would've certainly been better than the alternative. It crossed my mind to simply decline the call, but that would've made Rock ask questions.

"Hello?"

"You need to come out here ASAP," Justice said in greeting.

"Uh, I can't do that right now," I replied, surprised by the request.

"I'm *not* asking, Ebony. We need to talk face to face, so *get the fuck out here*," he growled, hanging up.

I could feel the heat rising from my cheeks to my forehead as anger consumed me swiftly. This nigga had *a lot* of mu'fucking nerve coming at me sideways because I was the *wrong* bitch for all of that!

"Who was that?" Rock asked, looking at me curiously.

In that moment I knew I had a decision to make and it was a simple as tell a lie, or tell only half of the truth.

"That was Justice," I replied, picking up my glass of orange juice to occupy my hands and mouth while trying to figure out my next move.

"Justice? What does he want?" Rock asked, putting his fork down and trying his undivided attention on me.

"He wants me to come to Cali for business."

"What business do you got with that nigga?" Rock asked possessively.

"Whoa, Mr. Jealous, it's not that serious and it's a surprise, so no third degree."

"Well you're not about to just jet off to Cali by yourself, so - "

"Don't even think about it, Rockafella. You're not stepping *foot* inside the state of California. Gangsta Bit may be dead, but that don't mean that you still don't have enemies out there," I reasoned.

"Fuck that! You're not going out there alone, so you either get that through your head or you forget about going," Rock replied forcefully.

The look on his face said there wasn't a chance in hell that I could win this argument, and that put my back against a wall. If I kept arguing, it would only make Rock more suspicious, and that could lead to a line of questions that I wouldn't answer unless I was at gunpoint. That only left one option.

"You're trippin', but whatever," I said, going back on my phone and arranging for my plane to be ready ASAP. After that, I went back to finishing my food.

"So what business do you have with this nigga?"

"Don't worry about it. You'll find out soon enough," I replied with attitude.

"Yeah, a'ight."

We finished our food in silence and by the time we got back to the car I received confirmation that my plane was ready.

"Take us to the airport," I instructed.

"Wait, we're going right now? What's the rush?"

"If I knew that, I'd probably know what he wants, but I don't so we're going now. You're free to wait at Ivy's house though," I offered, genuinely.

"Nice try," he replied, starting the car and pointing us in the right direction.

I still had no idea how the fuck I was gonna finesse this situation, but it felt like I was holding a live stick of dynamite while being locked in a safe. It was *all bad*! I had the good sense to text Justice and let him know that I wouldn't be meeting him at the Four Seasons this time around. Somehow that location struck me as an epically bad idea. His response surprised me though because he said he'd meet me at the airport. I wasn't quite sure how to read this demanded meeting, but at least now I had a way to keep Rock out of the mix. I waited until we were on board the plane and high in the sky before I put my plan into play.

"You know, we do have about three hours before we land," I said seductively.

"We do, huh? What do you think we should do with that time?"

"Why don't you come over here and I'll show you," I replied after pulling an in-flight snack from the drawer in my seat.

"What are you gonna do with that?"

"You'll see," I said, stopping him right in front of me before he could pull me out of my seat, and move me to the leather couch. I took multitasking to a new level by unzipping his jeans with one hand and pulling out his dick while using my mouth to open the Fruit Roll-up in my other hand. The look in Rock's eyes as I brought him to life in my hand went from curious fascination to giddy anticipation, and I knew right then that I had him. I carefully unrolled the fruit by the foot starting at the base of his shaft and working my way up to the head, until I had his dick looking like a delicious candy cane. And then I went to work.

"Brace yourself because I'm hungry," I warned, grabbing ahold of my snack with two hands and slowly taking my tongue on a tour around the head. Normally I would've tried to devour him quickly, but instead I took my time, inching my way down the dick until I had him snugly fit in the back of my throat. Two trips down and back had his knees rattling louder than the plane's engines, and his arms flailing around in search of something to hold onto. I was honestly enjoying this as much as he was because he'd never tasted so good. I gave him the *full* treatment, going from slow to fast, deep throating him, sucking the head like my favorite lollipop, and all the while refusing to let him cum. I was determined to take edging to a whole new level, so every time I felt his dick start throbbing hard enough to knock a tooth loose, I backed away and let him regroup.

"B-baby, *please*," he begged, after fifteen minutes of beautiful torture.

"Almost done," I purred, sucking the last remnants of the Fruit Roll-up off of his shaft. For the grand finale I went at him with no hands, grabbing him by his ass cheeks and forcing him to fuck my face until I felt his hot cum explode at the back of my throat, enhancing the fruity flavor in my mouth.

I didn't waste a drop, and when I finally released him from my mouth, he collapsed onto the couch behind him. I couldn't hold in my laughter or the satisfaction I got from seeing him looking like a fish out of water.

"I'm-I'ma do you in-in a minute," he said weakly.

He didn't even have the energy to put his dick away so I knew he was full of shit, but that's exactly what I wanted.

"It's okay, babe, I'll get mine on the way back. Get back in your seat and I'll wake you up when we get there."

He managed to stumble to his seat and strap in, and it was a quick ten minutes before I heard him snoring. Once I was confident he wasn't about to wake up, I got up and went to the back of the plane so I could call Justice.

"I'll be there in about two hours," I informed him.

"Fine. I'll come out on the tarmac."

"That's not a good idea. Rock is with me," I whispered, while looking to make sure he was still asleep.

"Why the fuck would you bring him?" Justice asked hostilely.

"Because you chose to call and *demand* that I get my ass to Cali, and he was with me. There was no time to fabricate a plausible lie, so I made the only decision that made sense. It's not a problem. Just meet me in the terminal."

"I'll be there," he replied, hanging up.

It had been my intent to ask him what the fuck was going on, but it was obvious he wasn't trying to say shit on the phone. Just as I was heading back to my seat my phone started ringing again, and I answered quickly before Rock heard it.

"Yeah?"

"Ebony, where are you?" Ivy asked.

"Uh, Rock and I decided to take a little day trip after my doctor's appointment and do some shopping in New York."

"You need to come back to the house," she demanded.

"What? Why?" I asked, picking up on her weird energy immediately.

"I'll explain when you get here. Have you heard from Justice?"

Right then I knew that something was more than wrong because she was asking about a nigga she didn't like, a nigga that I was flying to see as we spoke. Maybe she finally knew about everything Justice had been doing in the dark, and if that was the case was she trying to protect me or kill me?

"Nah, I ain't heard from him in forever. Why, did something happen to him?" I asked innocently.

"Listen, I'll explain everything once you and Rock get here. Just turn the plane around."

"Okay, we'll be there as soon as we can?" I replied convincingly.

My mind was racing when I hung up because one thing was becoming increasingly clear, and that was that whatever Justice had summoned me for had something to do with my former best friend. I went back to my seat and spent the rest of the flight trying to figure out what the fuck was going on, but I didn't have enough pieces of the puzzle to see the big picture. I'd hoped that Rock would sleep completely through the plane touching down, but my luck wasn't that good so I had to go to plan B.

"Wait on the plane while I go get us a car," I instructed once we came to a stop.

"I'll go with you, babe."

"No, you'll wait here because it won't take long, plus I don't know that you won't run into somebody who knows you in the terminal. Just hold still," I said, giving him a quick kiss and disappearing before he could argue. I texted Justice while I was walking, letting him know what gate I was coming through so we could make this quick and painless. To my relief, I found him waiting right outside of a Starbucks.

"Okay, I'm here, now what the fuck is so important?" I asked.

He took my hand and pulled me down a hallway that led to the bathrooms, stopping us halfway there.

"It's time for you to kill Soloman," he whispered.

Hearing those words made me understand why he'd refused to say shit on the phone.

"What happened, Justice? Right after I got off of the phone with you Ivy called, demanding that I come back to Texas and asking if I talked to you. Does she know what you've been up to?"

"Yeah, the bitch knows, and she already made her move. She killed my son and his mom," Justice replied, his voice cracking with emotion.

My mouth was open, but no words were coming out because I didn't know what to say. I'd had no idea that Justice even *had* a son, but I did know the pain of losing a child, and no words would fix what had been broken.

"I'm so sorry," I said, pulling him into my arms and holding him close. I could tell by the rigidity of his body that he was fighting to hold onto his composure, but I still wanted him to know that he could have my shoulder to cry on. We stayed like that for a couple minutes until he gathered himself and took a step back.

"I know you're hurting right now, and you know that I can definitely feel your pain, but are you sure you want me to do this?" I asked.

"I'm positive. I want you to go back to Texas and kill her dad."

"What about Ivy? You know she's gonna come gunning for us," I stated.

"No, she won't, because she'll be dead."

# Chapter 19
## Ivy

"Damn, bae, I thought you were coming back for another round by the pool," Big said, walking into my dad's office.

Given everything that had just happened I'd literally forgot about the good dick that had been waiting for me. I was too busy trying to make sense of a deadly mistake.

"Close the door and come sit down," I replied seriously.

I could tell by the look on Big's face that he understood immediately that something had gone wrong, but I doubted he was prepared for what I had to say.

"The calls from Manuel were to tell me that he was going to Mexico, and he'd be running shit from there with help from his top lieutenant over here. He also warned me against getting into any street conflicts."

"Why would he say that?" Big asked, taking a seat across from me.

"I thought it was weird too. Right after that call I got another call from a hysterical Darlise, and she was going off about some promise that I made her and broke. I didn't know what the fuck she was talking about, and she hung up on me before I could really question her. The next thing I know my dad is summoning me and asking if we have anything to do with a news story out of Oakland where a mother and son were gunned down."

"Wait, what? Why would *that* have anything to do with *us*?" Big asked quickly.

"Because the kid was Justice's son and his son's mother. From what I've been able to put together, Manuel took the info I provided, gave it to his people, and they went apeshit on the house thinking that Justice was inside. He wasn't -"

"Oh wow. Wow! This shit is bad, bae, but does it trace back to us?"

"Legally no, but it's not gonna be hard for Justice to figure out who made a move against him, especially since he knows that he made a move first against me," I replied, rubbing my temples to try and fight off the headache I felt brewing. This shit was worse than bad because an innocent child and mother had lost their lives for absolutely nothing. I hadn't pulled the trigger, but there was no way for me to escape blame, nor was there anything I could do for Justice to absolve me from what happened. Manuel might have wanted me to stay out of a street war, but he's damn near made that impossible.

"What did your dad say?" Rock asked, hesitantly.

"Well, he's pissed at Manuel for fucking up something that should've been simple *and* for putting me in a bad situation. With that being said though, he feels like I need to listen to Manuel's orders about not physically going to war with Justice myself. I already put in a call to Manuel and told him to have his lieutenant contact me *today* so I can see what his plans are to handle the shit show that's coming. I called Ebony and told her to get back here too."

"We can't be worried about Ebony and Rock right now. They're grown and can take care of themselves. Our focus needs to be on *our* next move, and to be real with you, I'm not with just sitting back and letting the Gulf Cartel be our first line of defense. They already proved that they can fuck up and I'm not about to let them cost us our lives," he replied with fierce determination.

"So what do you suggest we do, Big?"

"We gonna do what we know how to do. We gonna protect what's ours and kill anything that gets in the way."

The look in his eyes was that of a true solider, born for a war that never ends because there's always blood to be spilled.

I'd put my life in his hands any day of the week, and twice on Sunday.

"My dad's not gonna agree with us going at Justice," I said with certainty.

"You're probably right about that, and I mean no disrespect, but the decision is no longer his to make. What do you wanna do?"

Going against my father's judgment was still foreign to me, even though I'd been calling the shots for a while now. I understood that good business needed to trump everything else, but when the wolves were at the door, the only business that mattered was survival.

"Call a meeting. We need to meet with your people ASAP," I replied.

"I'm on it," he said, getting up and leaving me alone with my thoughts.

Despite going against what my dad wanted, I still felt like I was doing the right thing because nobody had a more vested interest in my survival than I did. Just in case he was right though I'd keep the next moves made to myself. Suddenly my secure phone started ringing and I knew it could only be one of two people right about now.

"Hello?"

"This is Juanito. I was told you'd be expecting my call," he said in a thick Hispanic accent.

"I was. When can we meet?" I asked.

"It will be a day or two, I have other business to finish first. In case of emergency you can call this number I'm calling you from. If I don't answer leave a message, okay?"

"I'll do that. I appreciate you calling," I replied, preparing to hang up.

"You need to remember what El Jefe said. Don't make any moves because we're gonna handle the situation for you."

It was on the tip of my tongue to ask him if they could do better than how they handled the last situation, but I would've been talking to myself because he was gone already. I'd been hoping that talking to one of the Gulf Cartel's top lieutenants would instill confidence in me with rewards to their capabilities, but I wasn't feeling nothing like that. I felt like Michael Corleone in *The Godfather* because every time I thought I was out, somebody kept pulling me right back into the bullshit. There was no use crying about it though. Instead, I took the time to reach out to Jeremy, Louis, and Roger so they would all know that it was time to take cover because a storm was coming. I didn't want them or their families targeted again, and I wanted all of our investments well-guarded. With that call out of the way, I actually had thirty minutes to myself to try and organize my scattered thoughts. It crossed my mind to actually reach out to Justice and explain that I never would've targeted a little kid, but I knew too much had happened between us for me to be believed. Getting him to listen could prevent a war, and I could only see one avenue to make that happen.

"You ready to go?" Big asked, coming through the door looking runway ready in a way blue pinstriped Black Billionaire suit.

"Go?"

"Yeah, go, as in into the meeting you just had me set up," he replied, looking at me like I'd lost my mind.

"Oh, right. Yeah, I'm ready, but we need to make a stop first," I said, rising from my seat and coming around the desk.

"A stop where?"

"Just come on," I replied, moving past him and leading the way out front to the car.

WHAT BAD BITCHES DO 2

Big didn't ask any more questions until we were on the road, and I knew he might not like my idea, but it made sense to me.

"So where are we going?"

"I wanna see Darlise. As far as I know she's still at the Hyatt, and I think I can convince her that I wasn't directly responsible for her nephew's death," I replied.

"I don't believe she'll hear anything you're saying based on what you told me. She's completely consumed by both grief *and* guilt because she may have wanted her brother dead, but she wanted those she perceived to be innocent spared."

"I know that, Big, but it's worth a shot because getting through to her can stop the bullshit with Justice," I reasoned.

"You *really* think anyone can stop him now? Blood cries for blood, bae. He's not gonna understand anything except that."

The truth in Big's words gave me a moment of pause. Maybe he was right and shit had gone too far to go back, but if that was true, then trying to reason with Darlise couldn't do anymore harm. When I pulled up in front of the hotel I didn't get out, but instead tried to figure out the right words to use.

"You sure about this?" Big asked skeptically.

"Yeah, I'm sure," I replied, texting her to let her know that I was downstairs and on my way up.

"You want me to come with you?"

"No, this is something I've gotta do alone. I won't be long," I assured him, stepping from the car and heading into the building.

The guilt I felt was almost stifling, but I pushed it down because the only emotion I needed to feel and express was remorse right now. During the elevator ride I worked on clearing my mind and preparing myself for a verbal onslaught that I knew I'd have to take without responding angrily. When

179

I got to her door I was prepared to knock, but the door swung open and I came face to face with a clearly angry Darlise. I'd expected that, but I hadn't expected the gun she was pointing at me. I didn't even have time to speak before blinding light exploded from the barrel, and my world immediately went dark.

## Chapter 20
## Ebony

"Come on, babe, talk to me, I pleaded.

"Now you wanna talk? Why the fuck didn't you wanna talk a month ago when you made a deal with the devil behind my goddamn back?" he asked heatedly.

"Rock, I told you that I did it to save you, don't you get that? Don't you understand that I would do *anything* for you?"

"Except be real with me, right? That's *too* much to ask, huh? You're my *wife*, Ebony, so there's no way you should be keeping secrets, especially when they involve a nigga you used to fuck!"

"I know, and *I'm sorry*, baby, I really am. Please just understand that I didn't keep it from you to hurt you," I replied, genuinely.

His response to my pleas for understanding was to go back to looking out the plane's window and ignoring my existence. After I'd left Justice and returned to the plane I'd had no choice except to come clean about everything – well, everything except the sex. Rock was pissed of course, but his way of showing it had been not talking to me or yelling at me, and then going back to not talking to me. I'd thought that his anger would be in large part for what I was about to do, but he didn't give a fuck about me killing Ivy's dad. He said it was just about me keeping shit from him, but I secretly believed it had everything to do with his perception that I'd treated him like a child. I'd bruised his ego, and that was gonna take time to get over.

"So where do we go from here?" I asked softly.

He didn't answer my question, but he at least turned to look at me before looking back out the window.

"Rock?"

"I don't know what you want me to say right now, Ebony."

"I want you to say that you still love me, and that we can get past this," I replied, fighting my tears.

"You know I love you, that won't change just because you do some dumb shit. And that means we can work through this and anything else. But right now I want to choke the fuck out of you."

"I won't stop you as long as you've got your dick in me while you do it," I replied, smiling.

This time when he looked at me his stare was blank.

"Too soon? Okay, I know I fucked up and I promise to *never ever* do that shit again. Can we please make up now?" I asked, getting out of my seat and positioning myself in his lap. I gave him my best puppy dog look before I started rubbing his ears, and kissing his neck the way he liked. He fought hard, but eventually he succumbed to me and gave me the toe curling kiss I'd been waiting on.

"I love you," I whispered into his mouth.

"I love you too, but you're still not getting no dick right now."

"You sure about that?" I purred, already reaching for his zipper.

"I'm sure. We've got work to do," he insisted, grabbing my hand and stopping my progress.

"Work?"

"Yeah, work! Or did you think we *weren't* gonna talk about you ending the existence of Soloman Black?" he asked seriously.

"Do you think it's the right move?"

"I think that with Ivy *and* her dad gone, it gives us the option to choose our own destiny and we can decide what we wanna do. The world will be ours, babe," he replied.

I definitely liked the sound of that, and I wasn't about to lose sleep over Ivy or her dad finally getting everything that they deserved.

"You're right, babe. The only real question is where do you want to go after it's all over? Because we still need that honeymoon/vacation," I said.

"I'm still down with your plans for Bora Bora, but don't think it's a vacation because you've got *a lot* of making up to do."

"Mmm, well I'll be sure to stock up on Fruit by the Foot between here and Bora Bora," I replied, kissing him passionately. We stayed lip locked for the remaining twenty minutes of our flight, and even though I was hoping for more, Rock was stingy with the dick. Once we landed I gave instructions to have the plane refueled immediately because once Soloman stopped breathing we were gonna reconnect with the clouds ASAP.

"I want you to grab anything we need and then wait for me outside," I said once we were in the car and headed to Ivy's parents' house.

"What if Ivy is there?"

"She shouldn't be, but if she is, then I'll kill two birds with one stone," I replied, smiling.

"Why don't you let me take care of this for you, and you can do the packing?"

"Because it's personal. She took my father from me and now I'll return the favor - hopefully with interest if I can get her too."

My mouth was watering at the thought of what was awaiting me, making me push harder on the gas pedal and bring the Aston Martin to life. Ten minutes later we pulled up to the house, but I was disappointed to see that Big's Rolls Royce wasn't there, which meant he and Ivy were gone. I'd have to settle for one kill. Walking into the house, we both went straight for the room we shared. Rock started packing while I grabbed the nickel plated .45 I'd inherited from my mother.

"Ten minutes and we're ghosts," I said, concealing the gun as I left the room and made my way to the first floor where Soloman was. Thankfully Ivy hadn't beefed security back up, and there was no armed guard posted outside his door to prevent me from entering.

"Did I catch you at a bad time?" I asked, closing the door behind me.

His eyes registered surprise, but I saw no fear in them, not even when I pulled my gun out.

"You know how to use that?" he asked in a surprisingly strong voice.

"You're about to find out."

"That still won't bring your father back, sweetheart. That's what you really want, right?"

"Don't pretend to know what I want, *Uncle* Sol, because you truly have no idea," I replied, moving closer to his bed.

"Don't I? I know you'd give anything for Jacob to be here right now, to take you in his arms and give you all the love you're missing. I know that because I know what Ivy suffered when she thought I was dead, thanks to your father."

"You can blame him all you want, but that's not gonna change what's about to happen here and now," I said, stopping at the foot of his bed and pointing the gun at his head.

"You're probably right, but if you think I'm gonna beg for my life, you're wrong. My only fear about dying before now was because I was worried that Ivy wouldn't survive, but now I know that my daughter can handle anything. She's built completely different from you and your weak-ass father, so while you think you're actually taking something from her, you'll really be doing her a favor and giving her a strength that last her the rest of her life," he replied, smiling widely.

"Her life won't be that long, trust me," I retorted, smiling too.

"You think so, huh? You're making the same mistake your father did in underestimating my daughter. It's okay though because that further proves my point and lets me know that we'll be dining together in hell soon enough."

"If I take too long, just order without me," I replied, squeezing the trigger twice and adding his brains to the wallpaper.

Even though I knew he was dead, I still stood there with my gun at the ready, secretly hoping he'd so much as *twitch* so I could pump more bullets into him. After it was clear that he wouldn't move in this life again, I moved towards the door, opening it to find Rock standing on the other side. I watched his eyes go over my shoulder and then come back to mine, searching with unconditional love to make sure that I was okay.

"Let's go, because -"

Before he could finish his sentence, his head jerked violently to my left as the sound of thunder came from my right. I tried to catch him, but he fell into the hallway, and the moment I went to step out the thunder continued rolling. My brain processed the information faster than my heart could, and I know I only had one option. As badly as I wanted to take Rock with me, I knew I'd be risking our child's life, so I did the only thing I could do and fired blindly in the directions the shots were coming from. Then I ran. I ran for my life.

*To Be Continued...*
What Bad Bitches Do 3

ARYANNA

The Power of a Queen

# Submission Guideline.

Submit the first three chapters of your completed manuscript to ldpsubmissions@gmail.com, subject line: Your book's title. The manuscript must be in a .doc file and sent as an attachment. Document should be in Times New Roman, double spaced and in size 12 font. Also, provide your synopsis and full contact information. If sending multiple submissions, they must each be in a separate email.

Have a story but no way to send it electronically? You can still submit to LDP/Ca$h Presents. Send in the first three chapters, written or typed, of your completed manuscript to:

LDP: Submissions Dept
Po Box 870494
Mesquite, Tx 75187

*DO NOT send original manuscript. Must be a duplicate.*

Provide your synopsis and a cover letter containing your full contact information.

Thanks for considering LDP and Ca$h Presents.

ARYANNA

**Coming Soon from Lock Down Publications/Ca$h Presents**

BOW DOWN TO MY GANGSTA
By **Ca$h**
TORN BETWEEN TWO
By **Coffee**
BLOOD STAINS OF A SHOTTA **III**
By **Jamaica**
WHEN THE STREETS CLAP BACK **III**
By **Jibril Williams**
STEADY MOBBIN
By **Marcellus Allen**
BLOOD OF A BOSS **V**
By **Askari**
LOYAL TO THE GAME **IV**
By **T.J. & Jelissa**
A DOPEBOY'S PRAYER **II**
By **Eddie "Wolf" Lee**
IF LOVING YOU IS WRONG... **III**
LOVE ME EVEN WHEN IT HURTS
By **Jelissa**
DAUGHTERS OF A SAVAGE **II**
By **Chris Green**
TRAPHOUSE KING **II**
By **Hood Rich**
BLAST FOR ME **II**
RAISED AS A GOON **V**

WHAT BAD BITCHES DO 2

By **Ghost**

ADDICTIED TO THE DRAMA **III**

By **Jamila Mathis**

LIPSTICK KILLAH **III**

By **Mimi**

WHAT BAD BITCHES DO **III**

By **Aryanna**

THE COST OF LOYALTY **II**

By **Kweli**

SHE FELL IN LOVE WITH A REAL ONE

By **Tamara Butler**

LOVE SHOULDN'T HURT II

By **Meesha**

CORRUPTED BY A GANGSTA **II**

By **Destiny Skai**

SHE FELL IN LOVE WITH A REAL ONE II

By **Tamara Butler**

A GANGSTER'S CODE II

By **J-Blunt**


**Available Now**

RESTRAINING ORDER **I & II**

By **CA$H & Coffee**

LOVE KNOWS NO BOUNDARIES **I II & III**

By **Coffee**

RAISED AS A GOON I, II, III & IV

ARYANNA

BRED BY THE SLUMS I, II, III
BLAST FOR ME
By **Ghost**
LAY IT DOWN **I & II**
LAST OF A DYING BREED
BLOOD STAINS OF A SHOTTA I & II
By **Jamaica**
LOYAL TO THE GAME
LOYAL TO THE GAME II
LOYAL TO THE GAME III
By **TJ & Jelissa**
BLOODY COMMAS I & II
SKI MASK CARTEL I & II
By **T.J. Edwards**
IF LOVING HIM IS WRONG…I & II
By **Jelissa**
WHEN THE STREETS CLAP BACK I & II
By **Jibril Williams**
A DISTINGUISHED THUG STOLE MY HEART I II & III
LOVE SHOULDN'T HURT
By **Meesha**
A GANGSTER'S CODE
By **J-Blunt**
PUSH IT TO THE LIMIT
By **Bre' Hayes**
BLOOD OF A BOSS **I, II, III & IV**
By **Askari**

THE STREETS BLEED MURDER **I, II & III**

THE HEART OF A GANGSTA I II& III

By **Jerry Jackson**

CUM FOR ME

CUM FOR ME 2

CUM FOR ME 3

An **LDP Erotica Collaboration**

BRIDE OF A HUSTLA **I II & II**

THE FETTI GIRLS **I, II& III**

CORRUPTED BY A GANGSTA

By **Destiny Skai**

WHEN A GOOD GIRL GOES BAD

By **Adrienne**

A GANGSTER'S REVENGE **I II III & IV**

THE BOSS MAN'S DAUGHTERS

THE BOSS MAN'S DAUGHTERS II

THE BOSSMAN'S DAUGHTERS III

THE BOSSMAN'S DAUGHTERS IV

A SAVAGE LOVE **I & II**

BAE BELONGS TO ME

A HUSTLER'S DECEIT I, II

WHAT BAD BITCHES DO I, II

By **Aryanna**

A KINGPIN'S AMBITON

A KINGPIN'S AMBITION **II**

I MURDER FOR THE DOUGH

By **Ambitious**

TRUE SAVAGE

TRUE SAVAGE II

TRUE SAVAGE **III**

TRUE SAVAGE **IV**

By **Chris Green**

A DOPEBOY'S PRAYER

By **Eddie "Wolf" Lee**

THE KING CARTEL **I, II & III**

By **Frank Gresham**

THESE NIGGAS AIN'T LOYAL **I, II & III**

By **Nikki Tee**

GANGSTA SHYT **I II &III**

By **CATO**

THE ULTIMATE BETRAYAL

By **Phoenix**

BOSS'N UP **I , II & III**

By **Royal Nicole**

I LOVE YOU TO DEATH

**By Destiny J**

I RIDE FOR MY HITTA

I STILL RIDE FOR MY HITTA

By **Misty Holt**

LOVE & CHASIN' PAPER

By **Qay Crockett**

TO DIE IN VAIN

By **ASAD**

BROOKLYN HUSTLAZ

By **Boogsy Morina**

BROOKLYN ON LOCK I & II

By **Sonovia**

GANGSTA CITY

By **Teddy Duke**

A DRUG KING AND HIS DIAMOND I & II

A DOPEMAN'S RICHES

**By Nicole Goosby**

TRAPHOUSE KING

By **Hood Rich**

LIPSTICK KILLAH **I, II**

By **Mimi**

**BOOKS BY LDP'S CEO, CA$H**

TRUST IN NO MAN

TRUST IN NO MAN 2

TRUST IN NO MAN 3

BONDED BY BLOOD

SHORTY GOT A THUG

THUGS CRY

THUGS CRY 2

THUGS CRY 3

TRUST NO BITCH

TRUST NO BITCH 2

TRUST NO BITCH 3

TIL MY CASKET DROPS

RESTRAINING ORDER

RESTRAINING ORDER 2

IN LOVE WITH A CONVICT

**Coming Soon**

BONDED BY BLOOD 2

BOW DOWN TO MY GANGSTA

WHAT BAD BITCHES DO 2

www.ingramcontent.com/pod-product-compliance
Lightning Source LLC
Chambersburg PA
CBHW070020260626
47159CB00005B/1894